# Rose of Light,
# Thorn of Darkness

By

Jeannette Haley

Hidden Manna Publications

## Rose of Light, Thorn of Darkness

Copyright © 2006 and 2024 by Jeannette Haley

*GENTLE SHEPHERD MINISTRIES*
www.gentleshepherd.com

ISBN: 979-8-9893588-6-1

Cover: Painting © by Jeannette Haley

Except where otherwise indicated, all Scripture quotations in this book are taken from the King James Version of the Bible.

Hidden Manna Publications
P.O. Box 3572
Oldtown, ID 83822
www.gentleshepherd.com

**Facebook:**
https://www.facebook.com/HiddenMannaPublications/

# Contents

# FOREWORD

You may ask, why write a novel such as *Rose of Light, Thorn of Darkness*? The answer lies within the pages of this book.

If you are one who has ever suffered the heartbreak of rejection, betrayal, loneliness, or fear, experienced disappointment from a particular church, (or religious leader), or endured great loss, then this book is for you. Perhaps you have been called of God, but find yourself in a situation which prohibits you from entering into the fulfillment of that call. Then you, too, may gain insight and encouragement from this story.

With this in mind, it is my sincere prayer that the Great Healer of hurts and hearts will somehow use this story, based on actual happenings, to touch the life of each reader.

---The Author

# 1

# CLOUDS OF DARKNESS

*Therefore is my spirit overwhelmed within me;
my heart within me is desolate. - Psalm 143:4*

The forlorn moan of a distant foghorn drifted monotonously into the Danza home. Julie Danza, a slender woman of thirty-five, stirred slightly under the white Afghan her grandmother had lovingly crocheted for her. The oversized couch gave ample room for Julie's small frame, and in the dim light it vaguely resembled a protective parent embracing a frightened child.

Fog, drifting inland from the motionless Oregon harbor, silently clutched the homes scattered across the evergreen landscape with its moist fingers. Julie was aware of this silent specter which pressed against the large living room windows and blocked even a view of the new home across the narrow, dead-end street. She wasn't really asleep, but neither was she fully awake. She tried not to think about the weather as she lay on the couch waiting for her husband, Gary, to come home from his job at the Dayport mill. Lately the weather had more than reflected her own gloomy mood.

Her mind reluctantly began retracing the events of the past few months. She and Gary had been married nearly four years. She had been attracted to his vivacious Italian personality and dashing good looks even though he was a full fifteen years older than she and had previously been married and divorced three times. She rationalized that none of his misfortunes were really his fault and that those women just didn't understand a sensitive man like Gary. At the time, a small insistent voice in the back of her mind warned her that a wise woman should seek the counsel of God before entering such a relationship. Besides, she had never loved anyone as much as she loved Gary—except for Paul, that is. And, Paul had been dead for twelve years.

The thought of Paul, her high school sweetheart, always brought an ache to Julie's heart. They had dated off and on for six years before he was drafted into the Army. Their relationship had been based upon a deep and abiding friendship which blossomed into love. Paul had been mature for his age and had taken on the responsibility of trying to provide for his widowed mother and younger brother and sister. He always showed respect for Julie, and their relationship, unlike so many others in their age group, remained pure. Tragically, Paul lost his life while serving in the Army in Germany. The entire incident had been shrouded in mystery, and to this day she never had an explanation of what had happened to him.

Julie pulled on the Afghan and tucked it tighter under her chin. The coastal bone-chilling dampness penetrated even the most secure and well-heated structures. She closed her eyes and tried to relax her tight muscles to no avail. Her anxious mind refused to retreat to another train of thought, and against her better judgment, she gave in to the persistent and nagging images of the past. *How I miss him,* Julie silently admitted to herself. *I loved him. He loved me, I know he did. Not like Gary who . . .* She suddenly opened her eyes and took a deep breath. *No! No, I mustn't think such things. It's too late. Paul is gone and Gary is my husband. Besides, Paul was of another faith and it wouldn't have worked anyway.* Julie forced her mind to consider the facts in a feeble attempt to overcome her runaway emotions. *After all, I met Gary in church. He seemed to be such a good Christian.*

*And he was so much fun when we first met. I really did fall for him and I've done my best to be a good wife. So why…?*

Julie's reminiscing was interrupted by the muffled sound of Gary's truck as it pulled into the driveway. Jumping to her feet, she neatly folded the soft Afghan and placed it on the back of the couch. Taking a deep breath, she smoothed her thick red hair. Gary's footsteps grew louder, and his presence could be felt as he neared the house. Julie positioned herself behind the door as her fingers gently pulled it open. Gary brushed past her uplifted face, apparently unaware of the unconcealed disappointment in her brown eyes. He stomped into the kitchen and dropped his metal lunch pail with a clatter on the spotless yellow counter.

"Hi, Honey," Julie heard her voice whisper strangely. "How was work tonight?" She felt a small shudder run through her body like ripples on a pond when a sudden gust of cold air moves across its surface.

Gary's lips tightened. Ignoring her question, he leaned back against the counter and folded his muscular arms. "Why wasn't there an apple in my lunch today?" He tipped his head to one side and waited for an answer.

Julie couldn't believe her ears. Straightening to her full five-feet-three inches she tossed a strand of runaway hair back over her shoulder. Her puzzled eyes stared for a moment into his penetrating gaze. Gary may have been Italian, but there was other blood there too—tough, rawboned blood from Belgium peasants who were hard-working people who had become rugged and practically indestructible from years of hardship and misery. His eyes were blue, cold, taunting, and strangely empty.

Julie took a deep breath. She instinctively knew that no matter what she said it wouldn't be good enough and the inevitable barrage of accusations and harassment would begin. It was a nightmare that repeated itself all too often. "I," Julie began, "I, uh, we ran out of apples and I wasn't aware of it until it was too late to run down to the store today." There! She had explained it exactly the way it was.

Disgust and contempt outlined every inch of Gary's countenance. Throwing up his large, masculine hands as if to say, *What's the use? You are impossibly stupid.* He sauntered off into the living room and dropped into an overstuffed chair.

Julie's heart began pounding wildly. The sound beat a loud staccato in her ears, as she tried to calm her jangled nerves. She fought back hot tears which threatened to spring to the surface and plunge down her cheeks, betraying the ache in her heart. Swallowing hard, Julie followed her husband into the living room and knelt down beside his chair. She reached out to him with trembling fingers and gently stroked his strong arm. Her anxious eyes lingered admiringly on his wavy, dark hair, streaked with bands of silver. "Honey, I," Julie prayed inwardly for wisdom. "Honey," she began again, studying his stony profile, "I am sorry about your lunch, but I suspect there is something else eating at you. Do you want to tell me what's wrong?"

Gary's eyes remained fixed in a glazed position. He stared straight ahead as if seeing something visible only to him. Deep in thought, he stood abruptly and stated flatly, "I'm going to bed." Julie watched him stride down the darkened hallway and turn into their bedroom.

Tears, which had been held in check for far too long, flowed down her flushed cheeks and splashed silently onto the pink nightgown. Somber echoes of the insistent foghorn penetrated the stillness of the night. Its sound seemed to be directed straight at Julie who sat motionless and silent in the Danza living room next to her husband's empty chair. Somehow the repetitious signal seemed to become hauntingly personal, warning her of impending clouds of darkness much more ominous than those which enshrouded the Dayport Harbor.

# 2

# ECHOES OF LOVE

*For I am poor and needy, and my heart*
*is wounded within me. - Psalm 109:22*

Cheer, riding on beams of golden sunlight, flowed through the open kitchen window and spread itself in crazy patterns on the countertop. Julie, looking more Irish than usual in her pale green robe, probed through the crowded refrigerator. "I've just got to straighten this out one of these days," she muttered to herself. "Oh, where is that jam? Ah! Here it is!" She pulled out a large jar of homemade jam with a flourish. Mornings were not the time to find Julie Danza at her best. Especially mornings which followed on the heels of a night of misery and unrest.

Julie gathered her wandering thoughts from the dark corners of her mind. *No* she told herself, *not this morning. I'm not going to think about anything that will ruin this gorgeous day.* She buttered two pieces of whole wheat toast, scraped scrambled eggs onto a gaily patterned green and white plate. Then, trying to make her voice as calm and inviting as she possibly could, called, "Okay, Honey. Breakfast is on the table!"

Gary grunted a reply from somewhere in the living room. Julie poured boiling water over a teabag and sat down at the round maple table. Gary walked around her chair, looked down at his breakfast and made a slight face. Saying nothing, however, he pulled out his chair and sat down. Bowing his head for a moment's silence, he went through the motions of thanking God for his meal.

11

Julie removed the teabag from her favorite China cup, wrapped her chilly fingers around it for warmth and leaned back in her chair. "You're not eating this morning? What's the matter with you?" Gary quizzed as he spread strawberry jam on his toast.

"I'm not hungry. Anyway, today I'm going with Ruth and Patsy to the Christian women's luncheon." Julie paused hoping Gary wouldn't make some crude comment. People who weren't around Gary for any length of time shrugged off his obnoxious and oftentimes cruel remarks as humor. In public Gary was usually always the "good guy" and the "life of the party." But Julie had discovered early in their marriage that much of Gary's joking was only veiled cynicism and anger.

"Oh, well, have a good time. I've gotta run. The boss wants to show me some new procedures at the mill this morning." Gary shoved back his chair, got up and turned back to Julie. His bottom lip protruded hinting of a pout. "That means then, you won't be here when I leave today for swing shift?" A slight frown dented his handsome brow.

"Well, no, but your lunch is already made and I'll leave out some leftover roast and salad." Julie was unaware her face resembled the look of a fearful worshipper hoping to appease an angry pagan deity.

Gary's lips formed a wry smile, but he said nothing. Julie followed him to the front door. He suddenly turned and looked down at her for a long moment, and his blue eyes, tinged with pity, lingered on her upturned face. She stood, waiting, longing, hoping for some gesture of affection, of love. Julie felt her heartbeat quicken as she waited for what seemed like hours. Then in one swift movement Gary's muscular body moved close to his wife, his strong arms encircling her trembling body. Closing his eyes, he parted his lips slightly as he pulled her toward him. In an instant everything inside of Julie melted. She closed her eyes and swayed toward him in a millisecond of ecstasy.

"Ugh! Gary! No! Why did you do that?" Julie's voice rose to a shriek as she pushed him aside. Gary's hysterical laughter rang insanely in her ears. He threw his head back and forth while he gleefully slapped his knees with his large hands.

"Ick!" Julie pulled a tissue from the pocket of her robe and wiped her face. She could still feel his wet tongue as it had glided up her face. "You are disgusting!" Julie turned and stomped into the bathroom slamming the door behind her. Gary's resounding laughter could be heard as he sprightly walked down the front steps and out to his pickup.

Julie faintly heard the truck door slam through the locked bathroom door. Finally, the huge engine roared to life, tires squealed and he was gone. She clutched the edge of the sink until her knuckles turned white. "Satan!" she screamed through clenched teeth, "You are not going to ruin my day! I am going to the meeting today, and I plan to absorb everything God has for me!" Tears welled up in Julie's already bloodshot and swollen eyes. "Oh, Jesus, please help me!" She grabbed for a washcloth, ran cold water over it and held it to her face.

Peace and expectancy for the day were restored by the time Julie had showered and applied makeup. Yes, she was going to overcome. In fact, something good, something wonderful was going to happen to her today. She just needed to figure out what to wear.

Julie believed women should look their best for their husbands, and had even confided this to Gary. However, even though Gary's salary was one of the highest in the small town of 4,500, he had explicitly instructed her not to purchase any new clothes. He complained to her that his first wife was always buying new clothes and spending his money foolishly on her appearance.

There had been no argument, only disappointment. Julie had excellent taste, due in part to her middle-class upbringing and partly because of her own artistic abilities. However, Julie firmly believed a wife was to be submissive to her husband in all things, unless it conflicted with the word of God. Therefore, since she had married Gary, she relied on the many second-hand stores and thrift shops in Portland, where she had been raised, to supply her with a wardrobe.

She selected a pale peach, cotton dress which accentuated her thin figure, slipped into a pair of white heels and surveyed herself in the full-length mirror behind the bedroom door. "Hummm..." she whispered, leaning forward to gain a better view of the end of her nose. There it was, slightly red. She best apply more powder to it, but that would hardly hide the fact she had been crying to two nosy friends who never missed anything and were likely to discover this bit of evidence. "Rudolph!" she muttered to herself.

Julie's mind momentarily jumped backwards to childhood Christmases. It seemed she always had a head cold on Christmas and her mother teasingly nicknamed her "Rudolph, the red-nosed reindeer." *Mother,* Julie thought to herself as she patted the needed powder on her blushing nose. *Catherine, my beautiful mother.* A slight sweep of sorrow mixed with love mirrored in Julie's eyes. How she wished her mother was with her today. But Catherine had long ago dismissed herself from any church or Christian functions. *If only she could see...* Julie's thoughts marched on in a familiar and oft repeated procession: *If only she knew that not all Christians are hypocrites.*

Julie sighed, picked up her handbag, poked around for the car keys, and made her way out to the waiting blue Oldsmobile. It was an older model, but sturdy and dependable. She opened the heavy door and absentmindedly slid behind the steering wheel. Thoughts about her mother were incessant now, demanding attention. *I wonder what she would think if she knew how miserable I am.* She turned the key in the ignition. The engine started, sputtered and died. She turned the key again and the engine sparked to life. *Mom thinks Gary is the perfect husband. She'd never believe me if I did tell her what he's really like. On top of that,* she reminded herself as she backed out of the wide driveway, *she'd just blame me and say it was all my fault.*

As Julie straightened the car, she caught a glimpse of their next door neighbor, Mr. Abbott, watering his lawn. He turned his bony face away from Julie's brief glance as if to say *I don't see you and it wouldn't matter if I did.* "Huh," Julie muttered under her breath, "I can't say as I blame him much for his attitude." She stepped on the gas and expertly maneuvered between a row of parked cars. "After what Gary did to the Abbott's," she continued as if speaking to an invisible passenger, "cutting down their sunflowers because they were secured with strings to our fence." She had been horrified at Gary's overt action and reminded him that Mr. Abbott and his family watched Gary and her go to church every Sunday. Gary had simply shrugged his shoulders as if to say, *Who cares?*

Julie leaned back and sighed. Driving was one of the joys of her life, especially along the ocean front. Often, she would pop in a Christian worship CD, lean back and conduct her own private praise and worship service. Today, however, was different. It was a short drive to Ruth's, and thoughts of her mother hammered her mind. *Mother!* Julie deliberately, mechanically fought to control her thoughts, bravely battling the rising tide of emotion which threatened to swallow her in an unwanted flood of self-pity. Fighting back tears, Julie straightened herself behind the steering wheel as she turned in the direction of Ruth's house. *Yes, I'll pick up Ruth and then we'll go get Patsy. I'm early, so if they're not quite ready, we won't be late.*

*Mother!* Julie's hands tightened on the steering wheel. Being an only child certainly had both its advantages and disadvantages. Lately she had considered trying to give up where Catherine was concerned, but she just couldn't do it. Trying to win her mother's approval had been a part of her since she could remember. Nothing was ever good enough; at least that's the way she felt. There were times when Julie almost believed if she could somehow earn her mother's approval, it wouldn't matter so much if Gary accepted her or not.

*Gary!* His name cut through her musings like a piece of sharp glass cuts through an unsuspecting and unfortunate bare foot. Tears stung Julie's eyes. She blinked them into submission and turned the big car onto Ruth's gravel drive. Suddenly it came—the unthinkable thought: *Sometimes I think I'm losing my mind . . .*

Ruth bounced gingerly through her front door before Julie rolled to a stop. A broad smile spread across her round Dutch face as she juggled her large Bible, purse, and notebook. Giggling, she opened the passenger door and pulled her ample frame into the car. Julie laughed. Ruth was always giggling and had a way of cheering Julie. Not that Ruth didn't have her moments of temper. Julie had called her the "flying Dutchman" more than once.

"What a gorgeous day! How are you doing? Is Gary working swing?" Ruth's questions tumbled over each other. Before Julie could answer, Ruth turned to her and squinted. "Rough night, huh?"

Julie's knuckles turned white as she tightened her grip on the steering wheel. Now was definitely not the time to cry. "Yeah," she answered hoarsely.

Ruth clucked softly as if to remind Julie she had warned her not to marry Gary. "He's not for you, Julie," she said bluntly. "Even if you did meet him in church, that doesn't mean nuthin'!" At the time Julie had felt shocked and hurt. Gary seemed to be everything a woman could want. He was fun-loving, handsome, hard-working, and attentive. On top of that, he encouraged Julie in her art career, making canvases for her paintings and special display stands for art shows. *No,* Julie had told herself then, *Ruth's wrong. Gary is perfect for me. We'll show her!*

Ruth's usually incessant chatter ceased and she drummed her fingers on the top of her Bible. Sensing Julie's fragile emotional state, she suddenly became absorbed in the familiar scenery.

The awkward silence was short-lived. Julie pulled the car to a stop in front of Patsy's small home where she was busy watering a colorful collection of potted plants. Patsy was a charming, petite young woman in her late twenties. Her thick, bouncy blonde hair shimmered in the unusually brilliant sunshine and her deep blue eyes sparkled with enthusiasm. "I'm ready!" she called over her shoulder as she disappeared through the open doorway. "Just have to grab my stuff!"

Patsy's presence in the car seemed to dispel the previously tense and gloomy atmosphere. The three women chatted happily about the luncheon and Julie's spirits lifted. She forced thoughts of Gary and Catherine from her mind. *Yes, this is a special day, and something wonderful is about to happen.*

# 3

# FORBIDDEN FRUIT

*The fear of the Lord is the beginning of knowledge: but fools
despise wisdom and instruction. - Proverbs 1:7*

Gary's foot slammed the accelerator to the floor. The three-quarter-ton Dodge pickup responded with a burst of speed. His eyes squinted through the dazzling light and his lips pressed together forming a tight line.

"Women!" he said to an imaginary companion. "Women!" he repeated. A half-smile parted his lips, revealing a perfect row of white teeth. He began to whistle "Up A Lazy River," slowed his speed and guided the green pickup around a sharp curve.

A tall smokestack sporting the letter "D" came into view. The Dayport mill had been the supporting financial backbone of the small Oregon community for nearly fifty years. True, Dayport sported a number of marinas and accommodated several successful fishing fleets, but everyone knew Dayport's survival depended mainly on the logging industry.

Glancing quickly in his rearview mirror, Gary suddenly turned the large vehicle off the main road. Gravel shot out from beneath the spinning tires as he maneuvered the truck up a narrow, one-lane road. Undergrowth, left undisturbed for years, crowded the edge of the abandoned road, promising to reclaim it. Branches made eerie scraping sounds against the truck as it lurched and bounced over rocks and thudded into chuckholes. Blackberry vines threatened to wrap their spiny arms around the dusty cab but whipped helplessly aside as Gary forced the sturdy truck up the ancient logging road.

Gary's thoughts, expressing themselves audibly, seemed to synchronize with the swaying vehicle. "Yeah, it's not my fault...Julie has asked for it...she spends too much time working in her art studio, and...even though it's right there at the house, she should sit with me...and watch television like a good wife."

He gripped the top of the steering wheel and leaned forward. Shifting the truck into second, he skillfully skimmed past a jumble of protruding logs. The narrow lane widened temporarily into a green meadow carpeted with a wide array of colorful wildflowers. Gary licked his lips and scanned the scene for any sign of wildlife. Satisfied there were no deer visible in the clearing, he shifted into third and continued his one-way conversation. "She doesn't even like my programs, especially football!" He spat out the word *football* as if no more explanation were required. Anyone would understand how offensive and unforgivable such an attitude toward America's favorite sport was.

The small meadow soon gave way to thick underbrush and second-growth evergreens. The thought of potential firewood lit up his face. His clear blue eyes appraised the trees and his mind catalogued which ones would be easy picking for a sharp saw blade and axe.

Gary's mood abruptly shifted as he commenced with his one-way dialogue. In low tones he hissed, "And she's so...so...easy! Yeah, that's the word; she's no challenge!"

He suddenly slammed on the brake to avoid hitting a young buck. Small rocks and dirt pinged against the truck and pelted nearby rocks and brush. The animal hesitated nonchalantly, then gracefully bounded across the rocky road and disappeared through the dense brush. "Whewie!" Gary wiped his forehead with the back of his hand. "How come I never even get that close to a buck come huntin' season?" He urged the hesitant truck forward and lapsed into a short silence.

The brief encounter, however, seemed to jar Gary's warped memory and spun him into another audible justification from his list of grievances. "Sure," he continued the recitation as if reading from an imaginary list, "Julie always goes with me when I go hunting. She even seems to enjoy escaping for a while from her work as a painting teacher, but how do I know she isn't just pretending? Nope! I'm sure it's all just a front. And that's the other thing…Julie secretly doesn't want me to hunt!"

The bucking truck shuddered and slid sideways on a section of washboard and loose gravel. Gary expertly brought the vehicle under control and brought it to a stop. Shifting to neutral, he flipped open the glove compartment, pulled out a comb, and quickly smoothed his hair. He flipped the comb back into the crowded compartment, and then rummaged through it in search of a small bottle of cologne. Finally, the elusive bottle yielded to his grasp. Plucking off the top, he splashed a few drops into the palm of his hand and patted it on his clean-shaven face. "There!" he said, slamming the small door shut. "All set."

He carefully guided the truck down a steep grade, maneuvered through a shallow creek, and then drove back into the dense forest. "And what's more," he began, through gritted teeth, "Julie ruined my fishing. Since we've been married I never get to fish anymore! So what if my ex-wife got my boat! It's all Julie's fault!"

Gary's tirade momentarily halted as he quickly shifted gears to accommodate a sudden rise in the road. "And my family!" Gary's deep voice rose over the roar of the engine. His eyes narrowed as he finalized his well-rehearsed list of complaints with disgust: "My four grandchildren may be rambunctious, but Julie could invite them over more often. I never get to see them anymore, thanks to

Julie! She's so religious! I suppose she'll be at that luncheon thing with her friends most of the day!"

Gary wheeled sharply to the left, spun around an outcropping of rock and slid to a stop next to a new Jeep Cherokee. An attractive brunette sat relaxed behind the wheel. She turned and smiled invitingly as Gary made his way to her.

# 4

# THE STRANGER
# AT THE BOOK TABLE

*Trust in the Lord with all thine heart;*
*and lean not unto thine own understanding. - Proverbs 3:5*

The Surf View Restaurant lived up to its name. Situated on the edge of a rocky cliff, visitors enjoyed a commanding view of the blue Pacific. It was one of Julie's favorite places. She never tired of watching the great swelling ocean as each wave mounted ever higher until it broke under its own weight, then rolled inland where it crashed and thundered against the unyielding boulders. Even now, as Ruth, Patsy, and Julie wrote their names on pieces of tulip-shaped colored paper, they could hear the faithful "boom, swish, splat" through the large open windows. The cry of gulls circling the restaurant's outdoor deck in their endless search for scraps of food completed the breathtaking seascape.

Julie abandoned herself to the friendly chatter of her two companions and the other women sitting close by. The monthly Christian meetings afforded her an opportunity to temporarily forget her increasingly unstable home life.

Lunch was served, announcements briefly made, and prayer given on behalf of the guest speaker. And then the tall, stately, attractive, wisp of a woman known as evangelist Barbara Weston from Sante Fe, New Mexico, stood to her feet. Julie's eyes suddenly riveted on Barbara as she silently made her way to the portable pulpit. A hush descended over the room. It felt to Julie as if an invisible blanket of holiness somehow covered them all.

Humility, authority, and anointing graced Barbara's every move. Even the simple acts of putting on reading glasses, opening the worn Bible, adjusting the microphone, and looking at the women evoked a feeling of reverence and respect. Julie sat erect; her hands folded in her lap. Every fiber of her being was alert, watching, waiting. *Waiting for what?*

Thoughts tumbled rapidly through Julie's mind, expressing themselves more as flashes of memory than actual words. A picture of herself at sixteen, alone in her bedroom when in an instant the presence of the Mysterious Stranger had come with love and power, causing her to respond with a "yes" to Jesus Christ. *Yes, I'll serve You Lord. Yes, I'll go wherever You want me to go… do whatever You want me to do.* She hadn't understood then that the Holy Spirit had drawn her, called her. The sacredness of the experience haunted her for years—haunted her as she made one terrible decision after the other. She hadn't understood then the difference between priorities and goals; she hadn't known how to line up the priorities in her daily life in this world with the goal of serving Christ. Julie hadn't known what to do, but she knew she wanted Him, wanted to serve Him.

And now she was shipwrecked on the sands of time much like the great rusting hulk of the *Sea Queen* which lay aground seven miles north of Dayport. There had been not a few occasions when Julie jumped in her Oldsmobile to escape from the raging storms at home and driven furiously up the small coastal road to the site of the famous ship. There was something fascinating about the *Sea Queen* as she lay tilted to one side. Over the years the wild and ruthless waves succeeded in imprisoning the aft of the helpless ship under tons of packed sand.

Julie, buffeted by blasts of wind, allowed her imagination to run free. With red hair blowing defiantly, Julie dreamed of the people

23

who had built the great ship from their own private hopes and dreams. She tried to imagine what it was like for those who sailed her across the unfathomable depths. *Surely they had high hopes, plans, fears. Some must have seen God in the awesome expanse of sea and sky and trusted in Him.* Julie closed her eyes momentarily and listened to the incessant language of the sea. One could easily imagine the eager waves overflowing their bounds, swirling and pulling the dry land and everything upon it into their treacherous undertows. She opened her eyes and looked longingly at the proud bow of the stricken vessel. The surf splashed and flowed around it, gurgling a mocking invitation to return to the sea. But the prisoner on the beach lay motionless as one long dead.

Julie sighed. *It reminds me of our lives,* she soberly philosophized. *Vanity, vanity. One day we're sailing along with high hopes, eager to live and love. Then, suddenly, something goes terribly wrong, and...*

Barbara's voice jolted Julie back to the present. She leaned forward, absently sipped her ice water, and listened attentively. This evangelist was somehow different from any Julie had ever heard before. She began to hang on every word as she felt the Spirit of God flow through the room, through her own mind and heart. Here was a true servant of God. She was more real, more...Julie groped for a fitting definition, more...no-nonsense. This woman, whose message revealed an incredible life of suffering and loss, had truly paid the price. Yes, Julie knew in her spirit, she was finally in the presence of someone who intimately knew Him.

The meeting ended and Julie found herself wishing it could go on for another hour. Barbara's message had been delivered with anointed precision; every word drawn from the heart of God. A prayer line formed as women moved forward to meet with the Master. One by one the awesome Spirit of the living God reached out to them, touching, healing, filling, and meeting needs. Julie caught a glimpse of Ruth and Patsy as they made their way toward the prayer line.

Julie decided to fall in behind everyone else. It certainly wouldn't hurt to have this handmaiden of the Lord pray for her, she reasoned. Slowly the women left the room or drifted to the book table in the back of the room. Julie felt suddenly awkward, ridiculous. She was practically alone with this servant of God Almighty. She wanted to turn and somehow melt into the crowd now congregating around a large woman behind the book table.

"Hello." Barbara's voice reached out to her. Julie stepped toward the evangelist's outstretched hands. She felt her arms lifting up and her hands reaching out to touch Barbara's. As gentle, eternal power enveloped her, her knees buckled and she felt herself floating on a sea of golden warmth to the floor. Time seemed to stand still. Finally, Julie found the strength to sit up. Barbara's blue eyes looked into hers. She smiled and gently said, "Shall we try again?"

"Yes, all right." Julie heard herself reply as she stood to her feet. Barbara prayed for her. Later, she couldn't recall the exact words of that prayer, but she knew the Lord had surely reached out to her in that instant, confirming to her aching heart that He would never leave nor forsake her, that He knew where she was, and that somehow it would be all right.

Dabbing at the corner of her eyes with a rather soggy tissue, Julie walked slowly toward Ruth and Patsy who were busy looking through several of Barbara Weston's books. Julie loved books and decided to purchase as many as she could afford.

Without warning Julie found herself looking into the merriest eyes she had ever seen. The heavy-set woman tending the book table, who apparently assisted Evangelist Weston, totally captivated Julie. There was something indescribable about her eyes. Julie stood transfixed. What was it? What was so mesmerizing about those eyes? She felt empty, devoid of life compared to the depths of joy in this woman's eyes. Who was she?

In that instant Julie knew she wanted whatever it was that made this woman so different. But who was she? Her name tag simply said "Rose." Certainly, she must know God. How else could those eyes seemingly convey such depths of joy and life?

Julie impulsively threaded her way through the tightly-knit group of chatting women. No matter what it took, she was going to discover two things—just who this woman was, and how she could see her again. Little did Julie know this decision would change her life, forever.

# 5

# THE LONGING HEART

*And now, Lord, what wait I for?*
*My hope is in thee. - Psalm 39:7*

It was Sunday morning and three days after the women's luncheon at the Surf View Restaurant. Thoughts of Rose flitted in and out of Julie's sleepy mind as she filled the teakettle and set it on the stove. "Yes, I'd like to get together with you sometime." Rose had told her, "But we have such a busy schedule. I can't promise you anything…"

Julie felt her heart sink. Her pent-up emotions threatened to spin out of control. Rose had looked at her with understanding and compassion. "Here," she had softly intoned as she hastily scribbled on a scrap of paper, "here's a list of where Barbara is scheduled to speak. Perhaps we can meet after one of the evening meetings and go out for a cup of coffee."

Relief mingled with a tinge of embarrassment flooded Julie's face. "Thank you! If my husband is working night shift, perhaps…" Julie's voice blended in with the loud exclamations of eager women at the book table. Rose had stepped aside to become engaged in a lively conversation with two women who seemed intent on out-talking one another.

"It's time to go," Ruth's hoarse voice rasped in Julie's ear. "Patsy's gotta get home and get ready for work. She's got the evening shift at the café." Julie turned reluctantly, gathered her belongings and walked silently out to the car.

Now it was Sunday and everything was back to normal. *Just what is normal?* Julie asked herself. *Well for one thing,* her mind replied in logical order, *normal means you are happy where you're at. It means things are progressing in an orderly fashion. It means you have a goal, hope, and a future. It is supposed to mean you and your husband are going in the same direction.*

"Don't you think you should be getting breakfast ready instead of sitting there day-dreaming?" Gary's gruff voice jarred Julie back to the present. She rose stiffly, and without a word walked to the refrigerator, opened it and retrieved a carton of eggs. Gary squinted. "What's with you? You haven't said a word." He clasped his hands behind his head and leaned back in the chair.

Julie's mind suddenly snapped to attention. If she said one wrong word it would have the same result as a single spark in a tank of gasoline. "I'm sorry. I'm just tired this morning." Without a moment's hesitation she went on, "Would you prefer French toast or fried eggs and regular toast?"

Caught off guard, Gary's stern countenance brightened. "Ah, French toast!" He rose from the chair, came up behind Julie, put his arms tightly around her, pinning her arms to her body. He began noisily kissing the back of her neck.

"Gary!" she exclaimed. "The butter is beginning to burn in the skillet." He squeezed harder causing her to cry out in pain, and then quickly released her. Anger pulsated in his cold blue eyes and a twisted smile played on his full lips. Julie ignored him and quickly moved the smoking skillet to another burner.

Spinning on his heel he abruptly left the kitchen. "Call me when breakfast is ready!" he yelled over his shoulder. "I'll be in the living room."

Julie moved mechanically through the kitchen. *I can't please him, Lord,* she silently prayed, *No matter what I do or don't do, he's not happy! What is the matter with me? I've tried so hard to be a loving and submissive wife. There must be something I'm doing wrong. Lord, help me! Show me where I'm missing it!*

"Honey! Your breakfast is ready!" Julie tried to make her voice sound nonchalant and cheerful.

"Well, it's about time!" Gary rounded the corner into the kitchen and sat down with a thud. Julie watched as he spread butter and syrup on four pieces of French toast.

"Sit down!" Gary ordered. "Have something to eat. You never eat breakfast!"

"Uh," Julie stammered. "I'm just not hungry in the morning. But I'll drink a cup of tea with you for a few minutes, then I have to run and get ready for church."

Gary grunted. She watched him devour the stack of French toast. He smacked his lips and glanced over at her. "Not too bad for a change." Then he chuckled to himself, rose from the table and left the room.

Julie sighed. *Well, at least he seems to be in a teasing mood.* She mused. *But I never know if he really means it or not.*

An hour later the Danza's were on their way to Sunday school. They attended a rather large church that was well-known for its excellent staff of Bible teachers and training classes. Julie regularly participated in the women's Bible study which met on Tuesdays, helped with outreach to the community on Wednesday evenings, and accompanied an older Christian worker on visitations during the week. Their church was, in fact, adamant about training and equipping people for ministry. This held a strong appeal to Julie, who had always longed to serve the Lord.

Lately, however, a certain strange undercurrent could be felt whenever Julie approached the leadership about her becoming one of the teachers for the women's Bible study. There were times when she felt as if she had galloped full speed ahead only to wind up in a box canyon. For years she had taken courses and classes in preparation for greater ministry, but now that she felt the call to go higher, the church somehow managed to block every move. Again, Julie began to listen to the insidious voice of accusation. *There must be something wrong with you, Julie Danza. Something you are blind to, but others see it. You'll never be used by God. Who do you think you are?*

Julie, looking fresh and attractive in an off-white lace blouse and turquoise skirt, pressed close to her husband. Gary ignored her and impatiently tapped his fingers on the steering wheel, glaring at a large motor home lumbering down the road in front of them. Julie felt her stomach tighten as he stomped on the gas and swung out from behind the long RV. "Gary! Watch out!" she screamed as a pickup truck veered off onto the shoulder of the on-coming lane. It skidded to a stop in a cloud of dust. Julie turned in time to see the angry driver waving and cursing out the window of his stalled vehicle.

"Aw, for crying out loud!" he sneered. "Don't scream at me when I'm driving!" His foot pressed harder on the accelerator and the car lunged forward.

Julie fought to suppress a rush of anger. She clamped her lips together, moved to the passenger side of the car and stared hard out the window as if trying to see something in particular. But all she saw were the heavy gray clouds that promised to block any ray of sunshine that dared to challenge their right to rule the expansive sky.

A leaden silence hung between them the remainder of the distance to the church. Gary pulled roughly into a parking space, jerked the car to a stop, grabbed his Bible, and slid out the door, slamming it shut. He stomped toward the church. Julie sat and watched him for a few moments. He was obviously ignoring the fact that his wife still sat in the car. Sighing, Julie picked up her purse and Bible, opened the door and tried to carefully maneuver her white sandals around a mud puddle. It was beginning to rain.

Julie thought, *Even heaven is crying this morning.* She held her Bible close and ran toward the glass doors leading toward the sanctuary.

"Good morning, Julie! How are you this fine morning?" The exuberant usher beamed with joy.

Julie forced a weak smile, "Just fine, Herb." *You hypocrite,* she chided herself, *you are anything but "just fine."*

Gary had already seated himself near the front. He always sat in the same pew. Julie found it amusing how the people seemed to sit in the same places every week. She slid in next to her husband without looking at the fixed expression on his strong face. She didn't need to look at him to sense his mood. Gary's attitudes could seemingly radiate for miles, charging the atmosphere around him with invisible vibrations of anger and foreboding. In the beginning, Julie would question him, begging for an explanation for his displeasure. Always the answer was the same: "I am not mad. There's nothing wrong."

The worship service began. Julie closed her eyes and tried to close herself in with God. She was aware of Gary entering into the singing with gusto. She glanced up at him and noticed the pious look on his face with disgust. *If only people knew,* she thought to herself, *what a hypocrite he is!*

Julie started when someone tapped her on the shoulder from behind. She turned slightly to see who was there. "Rose!" Julie's face beamed with joy. Rose smiled reassuringly at her as if to say, *I remember you and everything is okay.* Before she could say anything more, Gary poked her in the ribs. She looked up at him and saw his glare of disapproval. She gave Rose a quick smile, and turned to face the front.

Rose! Julie's mood brightened. She was just the encouragement she needed at this time. God was so good! She made a mental determination to catch her after the service, to try and find some small window of time when they could meet. A strange feeling of desperation stirred in the recesses of her being.

Encouraged by Rose's presence, Julie tried to hold Gary's hand during the message, but he made no move to respond. She withdrew her hand and clasped her hands on her open Bible. She tried to concentrate on Pastor Sorenson's message, but her eyes rested instead on the couple in front of them. It was the same every week, week after week. Mike put his arm lovingly around his wife's shoulders and Sarah would smile contentedly. Julie stole a quick glance at her husband. *Did he not ever notice Mike's affections towards his rather "plain" wife?* Something inside of Julie wanted to grab him and scream, *Why can't you treat me that way?*

Julie tried to force her wayward mind to pay attention to the message, but it refused to be corralled. She found herself thinking back to the man she had deeply loved for so many years. Why did he have to die? Was God not aware of their love for each other? They had been closer than one heartbeat. Paul was only twenty-three when the Army sent word that fateful day to his family. *On the other hand,* she thought, *we could never see eye-to-eye about religion. That's why we never married before he left for the service. God knows, it might not have worked out either. And now I'm in this miserable situation—but I do love Gary. It's just that he is such a different kind of person,* she told herself. *And, he's so different from the Gary I fell in love with and married. Oh, God, just what is his problem?*

Julie's mental wrestling was interrupted as the pianist began playing "Amazing Grace." She stood with the congregation and sang from memory. Finally, the service was over. Julie turned to see Rose, but she was nowhere in sight. Julie looked frantically around the sanctuary. *Why do I feel so strongly about Rose?* She didn't understand her own sense of urgency, but it overwhelmed her, consumed her.

Pushing through worshippers who gathered in tight groups to exchange small talk, Julie worked toward the back of the building. She was vaguely aware of Gary loudly laughing and joking with three men off to one side of the crowded room.

"The Lord told me to get up and get the gun...that Bob was going to kill me." Julie whirled around at the sound of Rose's melodious voice. Several women listened intently as the soft tone of Rose's voice rose and fell. Julie couldn't quite hear the conversation, but she *knew* she just *had to know*, just had to hear this entire story from start to finish.

Suddenly strong fingers wrapped themselves around Julie's arm, giving her a slight jerk. She nearly dropped her Bible. "Gary, what..." Julie stepped backwards, trying to catch her balance.

"Come on, let's go! I don't want to miss the game this afternoon!"

"No, wait. I have to speak to Rose." Julie tore herself from his grip, slipped through the circle of listeners, and motioned to Rose. "Hi, Rose. I've got to go," she stammered breathlessly, "but can you come see me, please? You will be here with Barbara for a few weeks and..." Julie hastily scribbled her phone number and address on a scrap of paper, handed it to Rose and waited for an answer.

Rose's eyes searched Julie's face. Julie had never seen such compassion in anyone's eyes in her entire life. It was if they saw into the deepest recesses of her heart. Momentarily she forgot where she was, that there were people engaged in noisy conversation all around her, that Gary stood impatiently waiting.

"I'll try. Honest I will." Rose slipped the scrap of paper into her worn Bible, and put her hand gently on Julie's thin shoulder. Then, once again, her eyes, not quite blue, not quite hazel, reached into the depths of Julie's soul.

# 6

# LOVE IS CARING

*For thou, Lord, art good and ready to forgive,
and plenteous in mercy unto all those who
call upon thee. - Psalm 86:5*

Five days had passed since the Christian Women's meeting at the Surf View Restaurant. Patsy McCall absent-mindedly reminisced about the meeting and the book she was reading by Barbara Weston as she prepared to participate in Julie's art class. Memories of meeting Barbara Weston and Rose Miller interrupted her concentration of the practical concerns at hand. She stuffed an assortment of worn paint brushes into a stained canvas bag and glanced quickly around the tastefully decorated living room. "There it is," she muttered to no one in particular as she stooped to pick up a large artist's canvas. "Let's see, what else do I need?"

Patsy loved attending Julie's painting class. It gave her a much-needed break from juggling being the wife of a prospective political candidate, the mother of two active boys, and waitress in one of Dayport's most popular cafes. Today was one of those rare occasions when Patsy could squeeze in some time for herself.

"That ought to do it," Patsy pronounced out loud with a note of triumph. She had earned a reputation for forgetting things when going to painting class, and the other students loved to tease her. Picking up her purse, canvas, and bag Patsy struggled out the door. A brisk, salt-scented breeze from the giant Pacific playfully tugged at her ponytail and threatened to lift the large canvas out of her grasp. She tightened her grip and hastily deposited her belongings in the cherry red Camaro.

Patsy's husband, Daniel, was gone for several days. She missed him terribly when his career took him out of town for lengthy periods of time. But their love for one another was strong and mature. Patsy had managed to read two of Barbara Weston's books during Daniel's absence. Every word had gripped Patsy's hungry heart. She laughed and cried through them both and couldn't wait to discuss their contents with Julie.

Patsy's thoughts turned to Daniel. She knew he would be home later in the evening. She wondered what surprise he had in store for her. He usually brought gifts such as jewelry, clothes, or flowers to his vivacious and fun-loving wife. Seeing her delight and surprise each time he returned home with a token of his devotion brought joy to Daniel's heart.

It had not always been this way between the two of them. Before they gave their lives to the Lordship of Christ, friction and dissatisfaction frequently plagued their relationship. Patsy tried everything from periodic flirtations with other men to involvement in the occult in a vain attempt to satisfy the longing in her soul. Daniel simply buried himself in his work and tried to block his wife's erratic behavior from his weary mind.

But all that dramatically changed the night they gave their hearts to Christ. It happened at a dinner meeting Julie had invited them to attend. The speaker that night told of his own search for meaning and purpose, and how miserable and phony his life had been before committing it to God. His words hung like golden apples in a room full of starving beggars. The mighty, yet gentle, Spirit of God descended on hungry hearts, wooing and drawing them with invisible cords of divine love. Daniel and Patsy rose from their table and moved forward as one; yet each had made the decision to follow Jesus independently of the other. As Daniel and Patsy invited the Savior of the world into their hearts, silent tears of joy ran unashamedly down Julie's cheeks. She had prayed long and hard for this moment of eternal decision for these two people whom she loved so deeply. Patsy and Daniel were now a part of the family—the family of God.

Julie's painting classes weren't ordinary painting classes, to say the least. There was always plenty of coffee, desserts, and time for personal counsel and prayer for those who desired it. A handful of the students ignored the added bonus of spiritual enlightenment, but came because they couldn't find any other art instructor in the Dayport area.

Patsy pulled into the Danza driveway. Before she could exit the car, Julie was at her side, helping her unload her vehicle. "Guess who's here today? I'm so excited! You'll never guess!" Julie's excitement surprised Patsy. The latter knew Julie and Gary weren't exactly living in marital bliss, and Julie's change of behavior piqued her interest.

"Who? I can't imagine..."

Julie interrupted. "Rose Miller! That's who! She wants to paint!" Julie's words tumbled out excitedly. "You remember her, don't you? She was with evangelist Barbara Weston, you know, at her book table!"

Patsy nodded in recognition and Julie eagerly went on. "Rose and Barbara will be in this area for a few more weeks; at least that's what I think Rose said." She lowered her voice, "Rose can't afford to take art classes, but she has such a..." Julie's voice trailed off as she sought for words, "Uh, such an anointing. That's it! Anointing!"

\* \* \*

Three hours later the students began cleaning their brushes and packing their belongings. One by one they went out the door, promising to return the following week. Patsy, who sat beside Rose, was obviously totally absorbed with the newcomer. Julie smiled to herself. She knew once Patsy spent time with Rose, she would undoubtedly feel the same way she did about her.

"Another cup of coffee, Rose?" Julie asked.

"I'd love it," Rose replied, "but I don't want to take up all your time. I know you have a husband and probably need to cook."

Julie held up a hand in protest. "Here's your coffee. And I have all day. Please, Rose, tell Patsy and me about your life. I mean, I overheard you say something about Bob going to kill you and…"

Suddenly tears formed in Rose's eyes. She stared at the steaming cup of coffee and cleared her throat. The atmosphere was charged with suspense. Then Rose began to share a story that neither Julie nor Patsy would ever forget.

# 7

# A TORTURED PAST

*Bear ye one another's burdens, and so*
*fulfill the law of Christ. - Galatians 6:2*

A heavy silence descended on the once busy art studio which had, until a few moments ago, resounded with the happy voices of would-be artists. Rose's loud sigh seemed to fill the room with mysterious and unknown depths of sorrow. "It wasn't her fault, really," Rose said in a hushed tone. She paused to sip her steaming coffee while Patsy and Julie waited breathlessly for the rest of the story. Rose closed her eyes and continued, "Mother was young and vulnerable. She was beautiful, lonely and…" Her voice broke as she reached for a paper towel left by one of the students. She held it to her face. Light reflected off her thick brunette hair in a shower of color and her eyes registered the agony of a broken heart.

Patsy's usually bright and sparkling eyes filled with tears of compassion. She gently laid her hand on Rose's arm. Rose looked deeply into Patsy's eyes in silent communication. Her lips formed an expression of appreciation.

"Anyway," Rose cleared her throat, drew in a deep breath, and, apparently strengthened by her new friend's gesture of sympathy and understanding, continued. "Well, like I said, Mother just didn't know what to do with twins. There was no way she could take care of us with Daddy gone.  Ralph went to live with Mother's parents.

They wanted a boy so he could help with the farm chores when he got old enough. I was," her voice faltered, "I was sent out to Utah to live with Daddy's sister and her husband." Rose began to sob. She folded her arms on the table and buried her face in them.

Julie lightly put a hand on Rose's trembling body. "Oh, Rose," she whispered consolingly, "Patsy and I understand. We are here for you. We really care."

Rose lifted her head and wiped her eyes. "I'm sorry, girls. This is so hard. You see, that man, my uncle, he…"

Patsy and Julie exchanged knowing looks. "You don't have to say anymore, Rose. We can guess."

Rose looked somewhat relieved. "Anyway, I had never heard of God, but I just knew in my heart He had to be real. I rarely ever heard from Mother. She never came to visit, at least not until I was about thirteen. I couldn't bring myself to tell her about…" Rose blew her nose and continued, "him!" Her eyes narrowed slightly and then she explained, "Mother always looked so sad and frail. I loved her so very much."

"What about the Lord?" Julie interrupted. "When did you find out He is real and that He sent His Son to die for you?"

Rose lifted her head and looked toward the ceiling. But the expression of pure joy which came over her countenance gave evidence she wasn't focusing on the fluorescent lights. Julie's eyes widened slightly in amazement and wonder. For an instant it seemed as if she saw some sort of glow, an invisible yet visible light around Rose. She blinked and shifted her gaze to Patsy. Was she imagining things, or did Patsy see what she saw, or thought she saw? *Surely Rose must be very close to God*, Julie thought.

If Patsy shared Julie's experience, she gave no outward indication of it. At the moment Patsy was busy digging around in her bag. "Julie, do you have a pen and something to write on?" Patsy blurted out. "I used to have some in here, but, well they're not in here today!"

"Sure, I'll get it." Julie smiled to herself as she slipped into the adjoining room. She was momentarily relieved to be able to step outside of the emotionally-charged circle which surrounded the three women. *This is heavy-duty stuff,* she thought to herself as she located a scratch pad and pen. Her thoughts rambled on, *I'm so glad Gary isn't here, throwing a wet blanket on the presence of the Spirit. I need more, more of God. And I know Rose can help me find Him.*

Julie was the type of person who truly carried the burdens of others. There had been times in the past when she had become completely involved with people in severe circumstances. She was a firm believer in entering into the sufferings and heartaches of people less fortunate than she. This not only provided her with a sense of purpose, but it helped alleviate the heartache and loneliness she often felt in her own life.

"Thanks, Julie," Patsy murmured as she quickly scribbled out her name, address and phone number. She handed it to Rose. "Please, please come out to my place for dinner some evening. Daniel and I would love to have you!" Julie noticed a neatly folded twenty-dollar bill inserted in the paper. Rose carefully put it in her billfold. Patsy urged her on. "What happened then?"

Rose seemed to melt into another world. She was there, physically, but at the same time strangely absent. Obviously, the years were but as days in Rose's memory. "Utah isn't exactly known as a fundamental, evangelical state." Rose chuckled. Her laughter was contagious and Julie and Patsy joined in. "I'll have to explain this some other time in more detail," Rose said as she glanced over at Patsy's watch. "I can see it's getting late." Noticing the disappointment on her friends' faces, she quickly added, "But I did get saved when traveling evangelists came through the small town where I lived."

Julie leaned forward, "But what about your ex-husband, Bob? I heard you say that he was going to kill you."

Rose hesitated. "That was years later, after my children were born. Bob professed to be a Christian, but he was controlling and demanding. It's a long story. Things weren't going well, and he was becoming attracted to someone else. He worked nights as a waiter in an all-night restaurant. We lived in Phoenix then." She frowned and continued in a hoarse voice, "Anyway, one night the Lord woke me up and warned me that Bob was going to come home and kill me." Rose lowered her eyes and stared at the drops of paint splattered on the indoor-outdoor carpeting. "So, I got the gun. He saw me standing with it at the end of the hallway. He simply turned and walked off." She raised her eyes to the ceiling and then looked squarely at Julie. "It ended in divorce. He threatened to destroy my children, my two daughters and son, if I fought him. I, I..." Rose struggled to control the rising flood of emotion. Her voice quavered. "I lost them. All three of them. Then I met Barbara Weston. We became friends and have traveled together ever since."

Patsy blew her nose and stood to her feet. "Oh, Rose, I'm so sorry. How awful! I wish I could stay longer and pray with you gals, but Daniel is coming home tonight and I have to go." She fumbled around in her purse and finally produced her car keys. "But, Rose, I love you and I know we will get together. I'll pray for you on my way home!"

Patsy hugged Rose, gathered her belongings and slipped out the door. Julie knew Patsy didn't want to leave, but the time had trickled away and Gary would be home any minute. She began to feel tense and fidgety.

Rose had risen to her feet. "I have to go, Julie. Barbara will be waiting for me. We have revival meetings coming up and I have to help her prepare for them." She stood still and gazed at Julie. Something in her compelling eyes drew Julie into a web of warmth, love, and compassion she had never known. Suddenly, she longed to have a real friendship with Rose. Her loneliness, so

41

long held in check, surged uncontrollably into Julie's consciousness, overwhelming her with desperation. *I must get to know her, share with her the innermost secrets of my heart.* The words rapped through her mind like hammer blows. *Rose will understand what I'm going through! She will understand!*

"Julie" Rose's soft voice cut through the pounding of Julie's mind. "I need help. I believe God has shown me I can trust you. Will you help me, please?" She had gathered her few things and was standing at the door.

"Me? Help you? But how can I possibly help you?" Julie stammered.

Rose's smile belied the sorrow in her eyes as she opened the door. Stepping outside, she called back over her shoulder, "I'll call you."

Everything inside of Julie seemed to be tossing and turning. Was God somehow going to use her to minister to one of His servants? Was Rose an answer to her silent prayers for help? Even as she pondered these things, she heard the unmistakable sound of Gary's truck lurching to a stop in the driveway.

# 8

# DAYS OF DREAMS

*For in the multitude of dreams and many words there are*
*also many vanities; but fear thou God. - Ecclesiastes 5:7*

Rain slammed against the windows of the Danza home and bursts of wind buffeted the gray siding. Julie heard Gary rummaging around in the den. "Where is that game?" he muttered aloud. "Aha! There it is!" Gary triumphantly walked into the living room with a checker board. He grinned at his rather surprised wife. "Hey, Honey, how about a good old game of checkers? Betcha you can't win!"

Julie set aside the book she had been reading. This was an unexpected turn of events. Gary was usually buried in some off-beat television show. Julie, on the other hand, spent her time painting, reading, writing, studying, or talking to friends on the phone. She rarely watched television. To her, it was a total waste of one's life.

"Sure, I'd love to play a game. And I'll beat you for sure!" Julie quickly jumped up, pulled her green sweatshirt down over her blue jeans, and followed Gary to the kitchen table. "Let me put on some tea water and I'll be right there."

Julie's thoughts and emotions played mental tag with one another. In her mind she tried to analyze why Gary was suddenly being so cordial. At the same time, feelings of love borne on wings of hope gave her a heady sensation. She stifled the urge to cry and giggle at the same time. Instead, she asked Gary if he would like some cookies. "Sure," he said absently. His large, strong fingers separated the red and black checkers. "There, I'm all ready to beat you good. I may even skunk you. I'm black and you're red." He rubbed his hands together expectantly and waited for Julie to sit down.

Gary maintained a cool but congenial attitude during several rounds of checkers. Julie was no match for his clever maneuvers, but she didn't mind losing. She had learned the hard way Gary didn't respond too kindly when he lost at anything. Julie knew that was the reason he never took her bowling anymore. She had soundly beaten him once, and that concluded any future bowling dates.

"You like that woman, don't you?" Gary's cold blue eyes stared hard at Julie over five black kings on the checkerboard.

Julie felt her heart quicken and her mouth turn dry. The last thing she wanted was another argument with her hot-tempered Italian husband. "Well, umm, I just met her, you know."

"There you go again!" Gary slammed his large fist down on the table. Checkers tumbled with a clatter and spread haphazardly over the black and red squares. "You never answer my questions right. I never get a straight answer out of you!"

Julie pulled upon an inner strength and tried to appear calm. "I'm sorry, Honey," she said quietly. "Yes, I guess I like her. She wants me to help her write a book about her life. Is that all right with you?" Rose had called her early that morning and posed the question to her. Julie was excited about the prospect of learning all the details of Rose's somewhat mystical life first-hand. *Besides*, she had reasoned with herself, *it'll give me an opportunity to serve the Lord, and right here at home, too. All I have to do is somehow get Gary to cooperate.*

44

Julie sucked in her breath and waited for Gary's response. His face had taken on the appearance of a bronze statute for a few seconds. It seemed to Julie as if hours passed before he finally relaxed. Letting out a loud laugh, he shook his head back and forth. "Oh, I don't care what you do. How long will it take?" His voice had a sarcastic note to it which made Julie feel uneasy. She tried to appear nonchalant.

"Oh, I don't really know, but it probably won't take more than three months." She watched his face intently, searching for any signs of displeasure. When she detected none, she went on, "And, she has to use my typewriter because she and Barbara can't haul a lot of stuff around while they are on the road, and Barbara took the laptop." Julie stopped and waited warily. She resembled a dog cowering before its master after a severe beating. She never knew just how far she could go when explaining anything to Gary before he blew up.

Gary pursed his lips and methodically re-stacked the checkers. Eyebrows raised, he appeared to be deep in thought. *No telling what he is going to say,* Julie thought. She put her elbows on the table and rested her chin thoughtfully on her folded hands. She had long ago given up trying to calculate Gary's thought processes.

"I saw Pete Farley today." Gary's sudden shift in direction startled Julie, but she made no comment. "The men of the church are going on a retreat. He asked me to join them and I think I will. Why don't you have that woman come stay here while I'm gone? I'll be gone a week."

Julie sucked in her breath. This was surely an answer to prayer! She never dreamed Gary would volunteer to go to a Christian men's retreat. And to think she would be able to spend time with Rose in fellowship and prayer! Why, this was the best news she had had in a long time.

For the next few days, the tension between Gary and Julie eased, although he avoided times of intimacy. Julie's relief, nevertheless, was obvious in her carefree and happy manner. She hummed choruses to herself as she did the cooking and housework. *Perhaps, just perhaps, Gary will find true and lasting peace and love at the retreat,* she thought hopefully. *Maybe God will change him into a loving husband.*

The day finally came for Gary to leave. He gave her a quick peck on the forehead, grabbed his bags and hurried out the door to the waiting van. Julie waved a silent good-bye, and then walked slowly to the kitchen. Loneliness stalked into the room and enveloped her soul. It could literally be felt like a giant monster pressing against her entire being.

Julie visibly jumped as the phone's loud ring punctuated the silence. "Hi, Julie." Rose's sweet voice reached through the phone, dispelling the gloom.

"Rose!" Julie nearly yelled. "I'm so glad you called! Gary just left, and I have the entire week here, all alone, and…"

"Would you like me to come over for a while?" Rose asked. Before Julie could respond, she added, "There is so much I have to discuss with you, and this would be a perfect time. In fact, if it's all right with you, I can stay until Gary gets home."

"Oh Rose, really?" Julie couldn't contain her joy. "That would be terrific! We can study and pray and everything! Can you come right now?"

Rose chuckled. "Well, not exactly, but I promise to get there some time tonight. How's that?"

"Terrific!" Julie exclaimed. "I'll be here with bells on."

For the next couple of hours, time seemed to stand still. The joy Julie had experienced was replaced by an invisible cloud of depression and guilt. The exuberance she felt over Gary's decision to attend the retreat was tempered by a nagging realization she was more excited about the prospect of having

Rose spend a week with her than the possibility Gary might be challenged by God to repent of his un-Christ like attitudes.

Through the howling of the wind, Julie's ears picked up the unmistakable sound of Rose's car pulling into the driveway. She flung open the front door, nearly tripping in her haste to help Rose unload her car. "Oh, I'm so happy to see you!" Julie radiated joy. She felt better now that Rose was here than she had in a long time. "How old is this car, anyway?" Julie asked as she lifted a box out of the trunk.

Rose smiled sadly. "Pretty old, Julie. Over ten years old, and it's probably the last car I'll ever have."

Julie wondered what Rose meant by that statement. It sounded so final. A feeling of sadness wound its way through her soul like melting ice water trickles down a frozen stream bed. "What do you mean?"

"Oh, it's all I've really got. I will never have enough money to buy another car! Barbara's been sharing this car with me, but she plans to purchase a new one for herself after we return home." Rose picked up a worn, blue suitcase and carried it into the house.

It didn't take long for the visitor to settle into the guest room. Julie always tried to keep this special room from becoming a catchall. Having a guest room for God's servants was an important and often overlooked ministry as far as Julie was concerned.

The two friends settled themselves in the living room with hot coffee, tea, and homemade cookies. "Yum," Rose said as she bit into the tasty dessert, "Gary is a pretty lucky fellow to have a wife who cooks as good as you do."

Julie hesitated momentarily. Rain tapped a steady staccato against the large window as the distant surf growled against the wet, cold shoreline. It was a good night to stay indoors. It was a good night to share secrets with someone she trusted.

"Rose," Julie began meekly, "I really am glad, I mean, really and truly glad, you're here."

Rose took a sip of coffee, then replied, "Julie, I know what you're going through. I mean with Gary."

Julie's eyes widened. "How? I mean, well," she stammered, "let me explain, Rose. I love him very, very much. It's just that..."

"He's abusive and insensitive," Rose finished for her. "Oh," she said with a wave of her hand, "I know how men are. Not that there aren't some good ones out there, but Gary needs to get right with the Lord first, and then he'll be able to do right by you."

"Do you think that will happen this week?" Julie asked hopefully, "I mean at the retreat?"

"We can pray that it does." Rose was looking intently at Julie. She set her cup on the coaster provided on the maple coffee table. "Julie, the Lord showed me something about you. Kind of a vision."

"No kidding?" Julie sat on the edge of her chair. "The Lord actually showed you something about me? What is it?" Her eyes were wide with curiosity.

"I guess it'll be all right to share it with you now," Rose said with a smile. She hesitated for a moment. Then her eyes held Julie's in a mesmerizing grip. Julie's mind seemed to lift into another realm, another dimension. It was like being submerged into a warm sea of security and peace. "Jesus showed me you are on the edge, nearly ready to fall off. I saw myself reaching out to you, lifting you up. But somehow it wasn't me, it was Jesus through me. Oh, Julie, it was truly beautiful."

Tears coursed down Julie's cheeks and splashed unchecked on her lavender tee-shirt, making abstract patterns of their own choosing. She wiped her eyes and looked over at Rose. "I know it's true," she whispered haltingly, "but I just didn't want to admit it to myself, or to anyone. I want this marriage to work. I really do."

"Then," Rose said confidently, "We'll pray together, okay?"

Julie closed her eyes. "Oh, of course, Rose, let's do."

As the night wore on, Julie became increasingly convinced that God had answered her cries for love, understanding, and help by sending Rose. Julie shared how the Lord had called her to serve Him, the frustration of lost years through wrong decisions, and finally her crumbling marriage to Gary. She told of how she had met Gary in church and how he seemed to be the right one. Rose nodded in agreement and sympathy. She wept when Julie wept and laughed when Julie laughed.

Julie lost all sense of time as Rose confided in her about her own walk with the Lord and her dreams of someday traveling the world over, sharing the gospel with great crowds of people. She related several prophecies she had received to confirm this calling. Julie was moved, challenged, and inspired. She hung on every word, captivated by the unmistakable spiritual presence around Rose. Julie wondered about evangelist Barbara Weston. Was Rose saying God was going to bring a separation, and putting her in her own ministry?

"Look at the time!" Julie exclaimed. It's one-thirty in the morning!" She stood to her feet and began picking up their cups. "Oh well," she said happily, "this is fun, and I'm not even tired yet!"

"Well, I'm a night person myself," Rose said brightly. Then just as suddenly as her face had brightened, a blanket of sorrow overshadowed her face. Julie noticed it immediately.

"What is it? What's wrong?" She set the dishes back on the coffee table and sat down.

"Oh, Julie, I haven't known you for long, and I don't want to burden you with it."

Rose turned and stared at the rivulets of rainwater as they raced down the front window.

"Tell me, Rose. I want to know what the problem is. Perhaps I can help you in some way." Julie felt strained and strangely tired and alert all at the same time.

"Well, all right, Julie, I believe I can trust you. But you must first promise me you won't breathe a word of it to anyone, even Gary." Rose folded her hands in her lap and looked imploringly at Julie.

"Of course not!" Julie promised. "I won't tell a soul. What's the problem?"

Rose sighed. "It's Barbara. I love her with the love of the Lord. I'd do anything for her. I can't believe what's happening." Rose choked back tears.

Julie leaned forward. "Tell me, and we'll pray together about all these things we've talked about tonight."

Rose's voice was so low Julie had to lean closer to hear her. "I won't have any place to go. You see, Barbara met these people from New York, Harold and Ellen Farnsworth. They, they just took over her life. It's awful!" Tears ran down her tan cheeks. "Barbara's such a woman of God. She has always had such discernment. I can't believe all this is happening!" Sobs shook Rose's body and she lapsed into silence.

"What do you mean you won't have any place to go?" Julie was alert now. No matter the lateness of the hour. She had to hear the whole story.

Rose regained some measure of control and continued, "When we are finished here, in Oregon, she is going to fly out of Portland and meet them in New York. They are taking her to Africa for some sort of ministry they have there."

"Wha-a-a-t?" Julie stammered. "I can't believe she'd do that! I mean, she is the best evangelist I've ever heard." Julie was visibly shaken. "What are you going to do? How long will she be gone?"

Rose slowly shook her head. Through trembling lips she said, "No matter what happens, Julie, I know God will take care of me. He always has. I'm going to serve Him. He called me to be an evangelist to the small towns and villages of America, and I don't want to fail Him. I've already failed Him enough. Who knows? Perhaps someday we could even minister together."

Julie's heart skipped a beat. "Really? You mean you think God would ever put us together? I want to serve Him so much. But, there's Gary…" her voice trailed off. Somehow the thought of Gary more than dampened Julie's spirit.

Rose, perceiving what Julie was feeling, quickly said, "It's okay, Julie. Perhaps Gary really will give his heart to the Lord at the men's retreat. All I know is, you do have a call on your life, and I want to see it fulfilled somehow."

After praying together, Julie and her guest finally bid each other "goodnight". But late as it was, Julie found herself floating in and out of sleep. She dreamed of preaching to great crowds of people with Rose at her side, emanating compassion and love. Each time she would see Gary's face, diffused with anger, glowering at her. Then she would awaken and lay listening to the distant roar of the ever-restless sea. The familiar sound seemed somehow strangely different this night, almost as if the haunting and sepulchral chorus reached out to her on wisps of swirling mist to warn her. Warn her of what?

# 9

# VOICES OF DOOM

*Pleasant words are as an honeycomb, sweet*
*to the soul, and health to the bones. - Proverbs 16:24*

The shrill ring of the telephone wakened Julie with a jolt. Gary had left for work at six o'clock a.m. and Julie, groggy from a week of late nights with Rose, had gone back to bed. It never ceased to amaze Julie that Gary had consented to let Rose stay with them until her book was finished. His attitude had improved immensely, and Julie was sure the men's retreat had something to do with it. Whatever the cause, he had not confided it to her.

The insistent ringing continued. She fumbled for the receiver on the phone by the bed. "Hello?" she mumbled sleepily. She lay back on the feather pillow.

"Julie? This is your mother! I need to talk to you right now!" The tone in Catherine's voice catapulted Julie's groggy mind from its hazy state into a wary alertness.

"Hi, Mom. How are you? Why are you calling so early?" Julie squinted at the radio alarm clock and instantly realized she had made a drastic mistake. It registered 10:15 a.m.

"What are you doing in bed this time of day?" Catherine's loud voice demanded an answer. Julie held the phone away from her ear. *Oh, Lord,* she silently prayed, *what do I say?*

"Do you hear me?" Catherine demanded. "I want to know what you're doing!"

Julie knew no answer would be satisfactory. She remained silent and waited. There must be some other reason her mother had decided to make this long-distance call from Portland.

"Julie, I have a bad feeling about that woman you and Gary have taken in. Something's just not right. Listen to me, Julie, if you want to save your marriage, you get that fat, lazy phony out of your home!"

Julie could feel both fear and anger pulsate through her entire body, draining her of life. In her imagination she pictured someone suddenly pulling a plug out of the bottom of one of the fishing boats moored at the Dayport Marina, causing it to slowly sink to the muddy bottom of the bay.

"Mom," Julie began weakly, "please try to understand. Gary doesn't mind her being here. She has nowhere to go right now and I'm helping her write her autobiography." She knew her words were falling on deaf ears. Once Catherine's mind was made up, there was no changing it. Julie's stubborn nature, however, now aroused, continued with an obvious overtone of irritation. "She's only been here for three weeks. It takes a lot of time to write something like this. And, besides," she continued before Catherine could protest, "Rose has been through a lot more than you'll ever know. It's painful and difficult for her to relive all those memories."

"Where's Gary? I want to speak to him!" Julie's fingers felt like icicles as she clutched the receiver. Shivers of fear flowed up and down her spine. She felt like a harp, helpless in the hands of an invisible apparition that was somehow cruelly obsessed with running its gruesome fingers repeatedly over the strings.

"I, uh, Gary went to work at six o'clock this morning, Mom. He won't be home until after three this afternoon." Julie's relief that her husband wasn't home didn't relieve the anxiety she felt.

Catherine would certainly find a way to speak with Gary. And it was only a half a day's drive from Portland to Dayport. She could pop in any time she wanted.

"Well, this call is costing me money." Catherine's voice had a strange tremor to it now. "Julie, listen to your mother. You are my daughter, and I care what happens to you. Ever since I found out about that woman from Ruth, I've been troubled. And," Catherine paused, took a deep breath and continued, "I had a dream last night. It was awful. I saw you in an insane asylum. It was filthy and you were laying on a narrow little bunk, crying. I saw a dirty blanket separating your bed from the others in the room. Your clothes were filthy." Catherine's voice rose and Julie detected a note of panic in it. "I saw a big rat in the room with you. Then a man came, jumped on the rat and saved you. Then I asked you if you wanted to come home and wash your clothes. So, you came home with me. Now, I have to hang up."

"Mom, wait!" Julie felt the need to explain. "Ruth is just jealous because I haven't had as much time to spend with her, that's all."

"I've got to go. Come see me. Good-bye."

Julie muttered, "Bye, Mom," and slowly hung up the phone.

The smell of coffee floated down the hallway from the kitchen and somehow gave Julie a small measure of comfort. Slipping on her robe, she walked barefoot on the plush white carpet. The room was tastefully decorated with quality maple furniture. Peach and green curtains matched the bedspread and other accessories.

"Good morning, my friend!" Rose's cheerful face radiated joy and comfort. "What happened? You look devastated!" Julie felt herself pulled by some invisible force toward the kitchen table where Rose sat drinking a cup of coffee. She let out a deep sigh as silent tears chased each other down her pale cheeks. Her tousled red hair gave her the appearance of an orphaned little girl who needed adoption.

54

"Oh, it's okay I guess," Julie said as she wiped her face on her sleeve and sat down. "I think a good strong cup of coffee rather than tea will do this morning." Julie forced a smile.

Rose got up and poured her a cup of coffee. "Things must really be serious," she said. "I know you don't really enjoy coffee." Rose set the hot brew in front of Julie. "There you go."

"Well, it's time I learned to like it," Julie said lamely, "Everybody else drinks it and when I go with my partner from the church on home visitations, they always automatically hand us a cup of this stuff." She gingerly took a sip and made a slight face.

Rose fastened her eyes on Julie's weary face. "Who called this morning?"

Julie waved her hand as if it was of no importance. "Oh, it was just my mother. She always upsets me. She doesn't like any of my friends and she doesn't understand that as Christians we live differently than the rest of the world."

Rose's questioning eyes took on a knowing look. She squinted slightly and leaned toward Julie. "It's me, isn't it?" Julie didn't answer, but her face told the whole story. "I thought so." Rose leaned back in her chair and stared down at her coffee. "I better leave. I can drive myself to Phoenix and stay with one of my daughters. They both have couches I can sleep on." Julie began to protest, and Rose put up a hand to silence her. "My being here isn't good for you and Gary. I'm afraid he's going to want me to leave soon anyway."

Sheer panic struck Julie like a lightning bolt. "No! No!" her voice rose to a shout. Rose had given her the only real meaningful purpose she had experienced in years. On top of that, Rose understood her, needed her. And she was learning things about God and His Word she hadn't ever learned before. No, she couldn't bear to give it all up now. Julie believed with all her heart her future and possible ministry was all linked up in some unforeseen way with Rose.

Julie also knew far too well the difficulties of trying to minister as a woman evangelist in the male-dominated church system. Her previous years of child evangelism and women's studies were behind her now. The call to come higher, to minister much like Barbara Weston did, was her heart's cry. She fought for control. "Rose," Julie choked out the words, "you are my real family right now, my sister. I mean, I know I have Gary, but, but..." She had never voiced what she knew deep in her heart. "But he doesn't really love me." There! It was out. Finally, the horrible truth hung in the air like ugly gray ash from a smoldering fire hangs suspended between heaven and earth.

Julie's bottled-up emotions surfaced, spilling out much like a geyser when it suddenly erupts to let off pressure.

"Julie, listen to me!" Rose's voice was gentle, firm, knowing. "I want you and Gary to call the pastor of your church for counseling. You've got to give it a try. I promise to call you and to write. We'll always be good friends."

"No! I can't live like this anymore! I want to travel in the ministry!" Julie was nearly hysterical. Why didn't people understand? Why did they have to call her and cause trouble? Why had Ruth called Catherine and gossiped? Julie rarely saw Ruth anymore since that day when she and Rose had visited the Dutch lady. Ruth, on that regretful day, had sat across the small square kitchen table from them, giving Rose what Julie termed her "fishy" look. Somehow Ruth turned her nose up at people who didn't meet with her approval. It had hurt Julie deeply. Ruth was one of her closest friends, but if she had to give up that friendship, then so be it. At least Patsy loved and appreciated Rose. Patsy saw the same thing in the Spirit that Julie did. And Gary, well Gary had somewhat improved since the men's retreat. At least he didn't yell at her as much as he used to. Julie suspected that could be because Rose was there. What would happen between them with Rose gone? Julie knew Gary was an angry man. She could feel it, boiling and seething beneath the surface. He took pride in controlling himself as far as physical violence was concerned, but nevertheless his anger lashed out at Julie, cutting and bruising her in other ways which couldn't be visibly discerned.

"We need to pray." Rose's determined voice brought Julie back to the present. Rose closed her eyes and uttered one of the most beautiful prayers Julie could remember hearing. How she wished she knew God like Rose did! A small measure of comfort and peace settled over her. Yes, she would call the church and make an appointment. In the back of her mind, she knew Gary would go along with it. After all, everyone knew Gary was the "good guy."

# 10

# COUNSELS OF ICE

*My tears have been my meat*
*day and night. - Psalm 42:3a*

Gary leaned back in the chair facing Pastor Sorenson's huge oak desk. He ran his fingers through his thick, wavy hair and looked up with a smile. Charm, innocence, and humility were written on every line of his face. Julie, who had just entered the cluttered room, grimaced slightly at his deceptive theatrics. More than once she had told him Hollywood missed out because they hadn't discovered him. She looked around for a chair, hoping to sit at a distance from Gary, but discovered the only available one was next to him. She walked slowly toward it and sat gingerly on the edge.

Pastor Sorenson put his long, thin fingertips together on top of the cluttered desk, leaned forward and peered over the rim of his glasses at Gary. Clearing his throat, he asked, "Gary, I want you to tell me, in front of Julie, what bothers you the most about her."

Julie's mind instantly replayed the scene which took place in this very office only three days earlier. She had met alone with Judith, Pastor Sorenson's wife. She was an intelligent woman, and Julie held her in high esteem. To Julie's way of thinking, something seemed to be lacking in Judith, however. She felt awkward, substandard and more or less unaccepted by the older and more experienced woman. Now that Rose was gone, she felt more alone, small, vulnerable.

"Tell, me, Julie, about your intimate relationship with Gary," Judith had bluntly asked.

Julie squirmed uncomfortably in the unyielding oak chair. "Well, it, um, I mean, Gary is cruel."

Judith narrowed her dark eyes and probed further. "What exactly do you mean by that?"

Julie sucked in her breath and let it out in one continuous stream of verbiage. "He licks my face, he won't kiss me, he pokes me in the ribs until it hurts, he runs his toenail down my leg when we're in bed and jams it into the bottom of my foot, he never says I look nice or compliments the meals I cook for him . . ." Julie ended with a sob.

With raised eyebrows and expressionless lips, Judith reached over the desk and dangled a tissue in front of Julie's face. "Thank you," Julie's squeaky voice sounded strange to her own ears. It reminded her of the noise balloons make when someone twists them into different animal shapes.

Gary's deep voice snapped Julie's attention back to the present. She wanted to run, to not be a part of the scene in this stuffy little room. She felt as if all the oxygen had been sucked out of the air and she found it difficult to breathe. "Well, Pastor," Gary looked calm and casual as if nothing were out of the ordinary. "She has, more than once, mixed my shorts up in the laundry and they came out colored instead of white. One time they were dyed lavender! And," Gary continued hastily before Pastor Sorenson could reply, "she doesn't pack the garbage right. What I mean is, I take the garbage to the mill to be burned and I like to have it compact."

Julie's eyes rolled toward the ceiling and then fastened on the minister's face. She couldn't believe what she saw. He was actually fascinated by Gary's ridiculous accusations! Julie nearly

59

pinched herself to see if she was really awake or living in some unbelievable nightmare. She felt peals of laughter echoing somewhere deep inside her. It was so hilarious, all these little, stupid, petty complaints. Julie wanted to laugh out loud so hard she ached. Instead, she fished around in her purse for a stick of chewing gum.

"Oh, I see." Pastor Sorenson's eyes were solemn. "Is there anything else?"

Satisfaction spread over Gary's ruggedly handsome face. In a serious, pleading tone he replied, "Yes, there is! She never cuts the butter straight. It drives me nuts! She doesn't cut the cheese straight either. But the thing that probably bugs me the most is she won't answer my questions!" Gary's voice ended on a note of disgust.

"You mean, don't you," Julie blurted out, "I don't give you the exact answer you want to hear! You're always backing me in a corner, looking for some excuse to get angry!" Her face was flushed and hot; her eyes full of fire.

Pastor Sorenson tapped his pen noisily on the edge of his desk. "That's enough, Julie!" he said sharply.

Julie lowered her eyes for a moment to regain her composure. When she looked up at the minister his steady gaze was appraising her. How could he not see the humor in this situation? Of course, a failing marriage was not humorous, but these ridiculous excuses for mistreating one's wife . . . "Julie," Pastor Sorenson's tone was level, unfeeling. His thinning gray hair and pale skin added to his image of a man who spent too much time indoors, away from the surf and sun, away from God's magnificent creation. "Julie," he began again as if conscious that Julie's runaway mind was behaving like a wild horse which refuses to be corralled, let alone roped and ridden into submission. "You have heard these problems your husband is experiencing in your home. You know, from the Word of God and from the teachings of this church, what your responsibilities are as a Christian wife. You must promise to do better in the future." He leaned back in his chair without blinking and waited for Julie's reply.

Flabbergasted, Julie's mind spun into high gear. Images of one of the women of the congregation who had been counseled to submit to her abusive husband flashed before her eyes. Julie's heart had ached for her when she last saw her. Her arm was in a cast and her eyes were shades of purple and nearly swollen shut. But she wouldn't leave the brute because the church told her to stay with him. And then there was the woman who was repeatedly raped with knives and chains by her neurotic husband. She, too, had been told to submit.

Something snapped in Julie. "What?" she spat out the word. "You've got to be kidding!" Julie's sudden outburst startled the two men.

Pastor Sorenson half rose from his chair, but then lowered himself back into it. Pursing his lips, he tried to control his voice. "Julie, let me explain," he said firmly. "The other day when Gary came in to see me, he shared some of the other things which have been going on in your home."

Julie's eyes widened. Would this horrible nightmare never end? Didn't anybody care for the truth? Her lips formed a silent *"What?"*

"Julie," his voice crooned, "I know about that woman, Rose."

Julie caught her breath. Just what did he mean by that? What did Rose have to do with anything? She had been gone for nearly a month, and besides, she and Gary were having problems long before she met Rose.

"Look, Julie," Pastor Sorenson's smooth voice took on a pleading note. She knew her face, as usual, betrayed everything going through her frantic mind. He was carefully searching for words now, hoping to diffuse any possible explosion from Julie. "I realize this woman became your friend, and you felt sorry for her and wanted to help her. But at this time, she is not good for your marriage. Now, it's my job to look after your soul, and even though she went to Arizona, I am requesting you to submit to me and my wife, as your shepherds, and to submit to your husband in all things and to forget ever seeing or talking to that woman again."

Julie flung herself out of the chair sending it to the floor with a crash. "No! I don't have to submit to anyone but Jesus Christ." Dodging Gary's attempts to grab her arm, Julie jerked the heavy door open, ran down the short hallway, past the sanctuary where she had experienced wonderful moments of communion with God and raced to the parking lot. Fragments of sentences darted through her spinning mind. *So glad...my car is here...so glad we didn't come together...so glad Gary had to work overtime...God help me!* She clutched frantically at her car door and dropped behind the wheel shaken and dazed.

She looked up to see Gary and Pastor Sorenson standing on the church steps, watching her. Apparently, they weren't pursuing her, but Julie had only one goal. She turned the key, and the engine roared to life. She had to escape, to find Patsy, to get away from these two men who would not listen, who refused to understand, and who were determined to put her life into a suffocating prison.

# 11

# A STRANGER CALLS

*My heart is smitten and withered,*
*like grass. - Psalm 102:4a*

The Cozy Cove Café was by no means as large and lavish as Surf View Restaurant, but the atmosphere was informal and friendly. Patsy McCall enjoyed her position as head waitress. And now that she knew Christ, her job took on an entirely new meaning. No longer was it merely a means of making money, but now it provided an opportunity to work in the harvest fields of the Lord.

"Another cup of coffee, sir?" Patsy's eyes sparkled with joy and life.

"Yes, please, thank you," the bearded customer smiled in appreciation.

As Patsy moved efficiently to the couple seated at the next table, her eye caught a glimpse of someone dashing into the café. She dutifully refilled the empty cups and then turned her head to see who had been in such a rush.

"Pssssst, Patsy, over here!" Patsy whirled. Julie was slouched in a corner booth.

"Julie, wha..." Patsy had never seen her friend in such a state. Her auburn hair was disheveled, her brown eyes wide with fear.

"Let me get you a cup of tea. I'll be right back, then we can talk." She leaned closer to Julie and said quietly, "My shift is nearly finished, so I have plenty of time."

Patsy turned on her heel and returned several minutes later with an assortment of tea bags, hot water, and a mug. She slid into the booth next to her friend. "Now tell me, what in the world is going on?"

Julie cleared her throat. "We, I mean, they," she lowered her voice to a hoarse whisper, "what I'm trying to say is, Gary and the Pastor are thicker than glue." A faint shadow of a smile swept across Patsy's glowing countenance. Even in the direst of circumstances Julie's ingrained sense of humor surfaced unexpectedly. Encouraged with the sudden sense of relief she felt by this opportunity to openly share, she continued. "At counseling session today, Pastor asked Gary what bugged him about me. And do you know what he told him?"

Patsy leaned forward, "No! He didn't give that petty little list he keeps locked up in that head of his, did he?"

Julie sipped her tea, and then put down her cup. "Oh, yes, he did! He listed the whole nine yards!"

Patsy shook her head in disbelief. "And you say Pastor Sorenson went along with that bunch of baloney?"

Julie looked at her friend in bewilderment. "Pastor didn't even so much as crack a smile! And on top of that, he ordered me to 'do better,' submit to my husband and never talk to or see Rose again!"

Patsy gasped. "You've got to be kidding! Submit to that idiotic set of standards Gary has? Never see Rose again?" Her eyes widened in horror. "Julie, let me tell you right now, you've put up with more from that man than I ever would have. He's verbally abusive, that's what!" Patsy bit her lip and stifled the urge to let Julie know what else she had observed about Gary Danza. Instead, she added, "Rose was good for you, Julie. She brought some joy into your life. So," she looked around the half-full café and lowered her voice, "what are you going to do now? Submit to them both and lose your mind or what?"

"I don't have much choice right now, Patsy," Julie answered. "I need time to pray, time to think. I just can't go on like this with Gary. Since Rose left, his behavior has been worse than ever."

Both women lapsed into a short silence. Julie sipped her tea thoughtfully while Patsy stared at the fleet of moored fishing boats. They bobbed gently on the water and tugged against their ropes as if engaged in some sort of ritualistic dance. But Patsy's mind was replaying the scene at Julie's house the day Rose left for Arizona. She had never seen Julie so glum and silent. They both helped Rose pack her clothes, some of which Julie had purchased for her, the unfinished manuscript, two small paintings Rose had done with Julie's help and a few other personal belongings. Patsy gave Rose enough gas money to make the long, lonely trip.

The only thin, thread of comfort which linked the three of them together was the hope they would see one another in a few months. Rose agreed to come to Dayport and the surrounding area if ministry opened up. Patsy and Julie promised to work on an itinerary for her.

"It was a bad scene," Julie interjected, breaking the silence.

"At the church?" Patsy's face was filled with genuine concern.

Julie nodded. "Yeah, at the church. I just couldn't help it, you know? Everything is piling up on me. I simply can't handle it anymore." She then relayed her quick departure from the Pastor's office.

Patsy's eyes twinkled. She couldn't help but find some measure of amusement at Julie's graphic description of the latest turn of events. It served them right as far as Patsy was concerned.

"Well, I feel much better now," Julie said as she gathered her jacket and purse. "Guess I'll go home and face the music. I don't have any other choice. The Lord will get me through this crisis, and," she added with conviction, "He's never failed me yet."

Patsy walked with Julie to her car, gave her a quick hug, and promised to pray for her. Both women knew that no matter how impossible the situation appeared, God was still in control.

Julie prayed all the way to their driveway. She pulled in and sat for a moment looking at her house as if she had not seen it for a long time. It stood strangely alone and silent. Julie felt a surge of relief. Gary wasn't home. *He must have gone out to cut wood,* she thought. *Good! That means I'll get a few hours of blessed peace before he gets home. I'll have time to play music, pray, and even do some baking.*

Julie was nearly to the front door when she heard the shrill ring of the telephone. Forcing the key into the lock, she pushed against the ornate door. It gave way obediently as the incessant ringing demanded attention. "Hello!" panted Julie into the receiver. The click of someone hanging up in her ear frustrated Julie. "Oh, for Pete's sake!" she muttered to herself, "I wonder who that was!"

She put on some classical worship to play and curled up on the couch. The old hymns soothed her mind and inspired her spirit. She closed her eyes, humming to the melody. "Oh Lord, how I need You," she whispered. "You are wonderful, all powerful, holy, and just. My salvation, righteousness, fortress, and high tower. Lord, give me wisdom, peace, understanding." She lifted her voice above the music, "Oh Lord, what am I going to do?"

Ring, ring, ring. The penetrating din of the phone startled Julie. Was it her imagination, or did it actually seem to be louder, more demanding than usual? *Sorry, Lord,* Julie thought as she stood to her feet and hurried to the phone. "Hello?" Silence. "Hello," Julie repeated firmly, "Can I help you?"

A female voice, soft but somehow cold and indifferent asked, "May I speak to Gary?"

Julie felt an odd sensation tingling in the pit of her stomach. "He's not home right now. May I ask who is calling?" Click! Julie replaced the receiver slowly. *No,* Julie silently told herself, *Gary knows better. We go to church together.* It was just her vivid imagination telling her that he could even think of doing such a thing. She was a good wife to him, taking care of his needs. He knew she loved him. She told him that all the time. Well, it was probably just a sales person trying to sell Gary insurance or something. Or was it?

# 12

# YOU KNOW, I KNOW

*But there is a God in heaven*
*that revealeth secrets… - Daniel 2:28a*

Gary Danza glanced at his watch, trying to make out the time in the dimly lit cab of his truck. *Oh no! It's past 10:30. Julie is going to want to know why it's taken me so long.* He tightened his grip on the steering wheel and pressed harder on the accelerator. Only one more mile to go and he would be home.

He had left the church shortly after Julie's flying exit from their counseling session and driven up the muddy dirt road to Misty Peak's summit. The rugged trail ascended sharply and then converted to a series of zigzagging switchbacks. Once he reached the top, he swung into a pullout and stopped.

The view from Misty Peak was breathtaking. Far below lay the blue Pacific, stretching from the far horizon to the beach where sea and land met. The rugged and uninhabited shoreline stretched for miles. Gulls circled lazily below the lookout. Gary stepped out of the pickup and stretched. Then he smoothed his rumpled shirt, tucking in a loose corner. His eyes fastened blankly on a fleet of fishing vessels far out to sea while his mind methodically reviewed the day's events. *Yeah, Pastor Sorenson saw what I have to put up with. He agrees with me. Women should submit to their husbands.* He took a deep breath. The air was cool and fresh. *Ah! This is the place to be,* Gary thought. He

Jeannette Haley

looked around hastily as if somehow sensing he wasn't alone. Seeing no one, he turned back to the panoramic vista.

"Hello, there!" Startled, Gary visibly jumped. He whirled to see who had managed to sneak up behind him at this isolated lookout.

"Brenda!" he gasped. "What are you doing up here?" A broad smile spread across his suntanned features accentuating the whiteness of his teeth.

"Well," she said coyly, "is there some law that says a woman can't drive up Misty Peak to enjoy the view?"

"But, where's your Camry? Have you been here all this time, watching..."

"You!" She said with a smile. "My car is parked up there," she pointed as she stepped up to him, "behind those trees." She slid her arms around him in a tight embrace.

"Glory!" Gary said as he locked her in his strong arms. He bent and kissed her full on the lips. "Oh, baby, I'm so glad to see you!" He caressed her slender body and ran his fingers through her thick blonde hair.

"Gary," she murmured between kisses, "how much time do you have? I mean, I have all the time in the world..."

"Oh, Brenda, I need you so much," Gary whispered hoarsely. He inhaled the scent of her perfume as he kissed her forehead, her nose, her lips.

"Ummm, Gary," she said in hushed tones. "Come on. I have a blanket in my car," She took him by the hand and led him through the trees.

* * *

*Darn!* Gary slammed on the brakes in obedience to the flashing red lights at the railroad crossing. *Darn! This train must be ten miles long.* He switched on the radio to a blaring rock and roll number. His fingers tapped impatiently on the steering wheel in

69

time to the music. *Oh well,* he told himself, *there's enough firewood in the bed of the truck to convince Julie I was busy all afternoon. After all, I really did cut wood up there on Misty Peak later today.*

The last car of the train rumbled past, the loud clanging bell and flashing lights ceased, and Gary romped on the gas. The pickup lurched and bounced over the tracks and careened down the bumpy road.

Gary's mind continued a replay of his active day. *Man! It's a good thing Melody had to work today.* His mind pictured the tall brunette. They had met on Misty Peak on more than one occasion even though they had other, more secluded rendezvous places.

As Gary neared the turnoff to their house, his mind switched to his wife. *Poor Julie. I really did love her quite a lot. But, like I told Pastor Sorenson, she just doesn't do things right. I'm very disappointed in her, and I hope she gets a clue one of these days.* He reduced his speed and pulled slowly into the driveway. Not a single light was burning, not even the porch light.

Gary's face dissolved into a pout. That woman! Couldn't she even be considerate enough to leave on the porch light so he could see to get in the door? On the other hand, Gary felt waves of relief that he didn't have to face Julie tonight. He needed a chance to wash any trace of Brenda's perfume from his skin and beef up his alibi.

* * *

Morning came early for Julie. She slid quietly out of bed, cast a furtive glance at her sleeping husband, and walked quietly to the bathroom. Once inside, she leaned forward to look in the mirror. Two tired, brown eyes looked sadly back at her. She splashed cold water over her smooth complexion and cleaned her teeth. By the time she had tamed her long red hair into a single braid on top of her head, she felt more alive.

*It's Sunday,* she told herself as she stepped into the kitchen and made coffee for Gary, *and now you have to go through all the motions of getting ready for church, going to church, sitting through church and then confronting Gary after church...*Confrontation!

A chill suddenly coursed through her body, causing her to shiver involuntarily. Yes! That was it! The dream! God had shown her last night in a dream everything, except she couldn't remember seeing any details. But then, God is holy, and He would never show the details of something like that.

She hurried back into the bedroom and quietly picked out something to wear, then quickly showered and dressed. By the time she exited the bathroom, Gary was sitting glumly in the living room with a cup of coffee.

"Huh!" he grunted as he looked her up and down. Then in a more congenial tone he added, "How are you this morning?"

"Very well, really," Julie said firmly. She turned and walked into the kitchen. She glanced at the clock. "We'll just have time to grab a piece of toast I'm afraid, Gary, or we'll be late for church."

"Oh, I suppose so," he growled as he got up from the chair and sauntered to the bedroom. "Oh, by the way," he called from the other room, "I got lots of firewood for us yesterday." His comment was met with silence. He shrugged and stared in the closet, looking for something to put on for church. Something nagged at the back of his mind, bothering him. What was it? Oh, yes, predictable Julie hadn't called him "honey" this morning. Neither had she answered him when he announced they had more firewood. What could this mean? How could she possibly suspect anything? He was expert at changing images, and he had covered his tracks well. No, he must just be tired and edgy. Julie had no way of knowing…

71

By the time the Danza's arrived in church, the service had already begun. Gary looked at his wife out of the corner of his eye. Julie hadn't spoken a word to him all the way to church. But then, he reasoned, that could be because of their unsuccessful meeting with the pastor. *Yeah, that must be it*, he confidently told himself, *she's just mad because she has to knuckle under.*

Julie threw herself with gusto into singing praises to the Lord. She closed her eyes and worshipped Him with everything she had. Gary tried to imitate her and the other worshippers, but Julie heard snatches of His repetitious chanting and, annoyed, tried to close his voice out of her mind.

Pastor Sorenson stepped up behind the pulpit. His gaze swept the congregation and came to rest for a moment upon Gary and Julie. Her face, set like flint, unblinkingly returned his stony stare. He cleared his throat and closed his eyes. After a brief prayer, he opened his Bible to Genesis. "This morning, dear brothers and sisters," he forced a weak smile, "we are going to begin with Adam and Eve."

Julie's heart gave a slight jump. *Oh boy,* she thought, *here we go again. Putting the blame on Eve for all the world's ills so all of us women today will crawl out of here in shame.* Julie tugged on the hem of her skirt and opened her Bible to Romans 5. Gary glanced down at her open Bible and raised a questioning eyebrow. What was Julie doing?

"Yes," the pastor intoned, "God gave the first couple everything they had need of. But you will notice, Eve wasn't content. No, she was discontented, unthankful, and rebellious." His eyes locked with Julie's and then he retreated to the safety of His Bible. Julie unflinchingly shot daggers at him. It was not because she was personally put out with the man. No, it was much more than that. He was twisting scripture, and nothing rankled her more than somebody messing around with God's word.

Determined to nail down the proper role of women in the church, Pastor Sorenson relentlessly trudged down the trail of error. Julie's face registered her disgust. She glanced around the sanctuary, hoping to find at least two or three women who disagreed with him. She noticed Patsy in the back of the church, listening soberly. Julie thought she saw anger smoldering in her beautiful eyes. *That's a good sign,* Julie thought. She looked to the front and saw Judith. She sat with her head bowed as if in total reverence and submission to her pastor husband. Judith reminded Julie of a whipped puppy. Finally, she spotted Mary, the woman who had taught Julie so much and with whom she frequently made house calls. They had ministered together a lot over the years. Julie nearly groaned out loud at what she saw. Mary sat, eyes closed, in rapt attention, swallowing every word Pastor Sorenson spoke.

"Therefore," the preacher's voice rose, "women are to be under the rule of their husbands. For through the sins and transgressions of Eve man was drawn into the destructive powers of sin."

*What about husbands loving their wives as Jesus loves the church?* Julie silently argued. *What about verse twelve of Romans chapter five which plainly tells us that through one man, not woman, sin and death entered into the world?* She looked up into the expressionless face of Pastor Sorenson. His eyes glittered with a strange kind of power. He looked at her triumphantly.

Julie shook her head slightly in an unspoken, *No, you are all wrong* and tapped her finger on her open Bible. He colored slightly and shifted his gaze to the back of the room. "So, it is the duty of women according to the word of God to come under their husband's authority. To come out from under the chain of command is to be removed from God's protection!"

Julie cleared her throat. She wanted to jump up and point at the preacher and rebuke him for putting women in a position God never intended for them to be in. Who did he think he was? She closed her eyes, trying to shut out the subtle but erroneous words. She felt dizzy, sick. Women were to submit to the Lord first and then their husbands as unto the Lord. Their husbands were to love them, not lord it over them.

Suddenly she found herself standing to her feet, Bible and purse in hand. She stumbled past three people sitting between her and the closest aisle and walked briskly to the back of the church, out through the open door, into the foyer, past the surprised ushers, and out the main entrance.

"Hey, wait up!" Surprised, Julie turned to see Patsy hurrying to her side. "What a bunch of unbiblical poppycock!" She tossed her bouncy hair and smiled at Julie's strained face.

"Boy, you've sure got that right!" Julie stated. "Let's go sit in your car and wait until it's over with."

"Sure." Patsy led her through the maze of parked cars to her Camaro. "Daniel is gone again on a trip and the boys are at camp. So, I thought I'd just come this morning to see what's happening."

"Thanks," Julie whispered gratefully. "I appreciate you so much, Patsy. What would I do without you?"

"Ah, you'd do okay. Hey, have you heard from Rose lately?"

"Well, no." Julie's eyes looked strangely forlorn. Patsy knew there was more to it than not hearing from their friend.

"What happened last night? I mean, what did Gary say?" Patsy cocked her head to one side and waited for an answer.

"Nothing."

"Nothing? After all that happened here at that so-called counseling session?"

Julie sighed. "He wasn't home when I got there, Patsy. In fact, I was in bed asleep when he finally showed up. Perhaps that's just as well. That way, we didn't have to get into a big discussion which would only end up in a fight."

Patsy's brow furrowed as she sat deep in thought.  Finally, she spoke, "Uh, Julie, where did he go?  I mean, what was he doing until late at night?"

Tears filled Julie's eyes. "Well, he brought home some firewood.  That's all he would tell me." She pulled a tissue out of her purse and dabbed at her eyes. "Patsy, there were two phone calls yesterday. The first one, the caller hung up. But the second one, well, it was a woman's voice asking for Gary."

Patsy leaned forward. "Julie," she said slowly, "are you saying you think he is seeing another woman or something like that?  I mean, how can you come to that conclusion from a phone call?"

"I know it, Patsy."

"What! Since when, I mean, how come you didn't tell me about that yesterday?  I mean, did you discover something last night or what?"

"No, I didn't discover anything.  But God showed me…"

Suddenly the car began rocking violently as someone shoved against it.  Both women turned as one to look out the back window. Gary, his large hands on the trunk, bounced the car up and down.

"It's Gary. I've got to go. I'll call you or come to the café. Honest. Bye!"

Before the surprised Patsy could reply, Julie had exited the car and was following Gary through the busy parking lot to their car.

"So!  You just had to make a fool of me and stomp out of the church like some insipid little kid!" Gary's face was livid with anger.

"He's preaching heresy and I don't have to listen to it!" Julie shot back. "And furthermore, if all those mesmerized people really loved the truth, they wouldn't stand for it either!"

"Oh, so I'm mesmerized, am I?" He turned the key in the ignition and stomped on the gas. The car lurched forward and died.

"Do you have to treat my car so rough?" Julie's voice had risen to match his.

"If you don't like the way I drive, then drive yourself." He threw the door open, climbed out, slammed the door and stomped around the car to the passenger side. Opening the door, he yelled, "Get out and get behind the wheel!"

Julie unsnapped her seatbelt, swung out of the car, stomped around to the driver's seat and started the car. It roared to life and she pulled out onto the street.

"Hey! Where are you going?" Gary sneered.

"We are going for a ride. I've got something to say."

"Oh, you do, do you? Like what?"

"Like," she paused, praying for the right answers, "I know what you've been doing."

Gary's face blanched. "Oh? Just what have I been doing?"

"Committing adultery." Julie's tone was strong, even, and decisive. Her statement went through him like a sword. There would be no argument. He knew by her calm demeanor and the tone of her voice that the game was up. He wasn't sure who had won and who had lost, but there could be no denying it. Julie knew.

"Yes," he said without emotion and then added, "Who did you say told you?"

"God." Julie stated matter-of-factly. She slowed the car and did a U-turn. Neither spoke a word the rest of the way home. Gary sat slouched on his side of the car. When they arrived home, he quickly exited the car, opened the front door, and went to their bedroom.

Julie strode into the kitchen and leaned against the counter for support. Her body trembled with the shock of it all, but she tried to remain calm. *I must not weaken now. I must stay strong, rational. I need You to walk me through this, Lord.* She didn't know how long she stood there when Gary walked into the kitchen. He ran his fingers nervously through his hair. His face was an emotionless mask, but she could tell he was struggling.

"Will you forgive me?" he said without feeling.

"Yes, as a Christian, I forgive you," Julie said through gritted teeth. She knew she must forgive, that it was necessary for her to forgive. Regardless of how she felt about it, with God's help, she would forgive.

Gary heaved a sigh of relief. He turned and walked into the living room and flipped on the television. The blare of the football game permeated the house and crashed against Julie's tired mind. She could hear him over the din making comments to the players.

*I can't stand this,* she thought. *I'm losing my mind. I have to get out of here.* She wanted to run, but instead forced herself to walk normally to the bedroom so she could change into her blue jeans and sweatshirt. "I'm going out, Gary," she said as she walked past his chair to the front door.

"Uh, oh. Where are you going?" Gary squinted up at her.

"Just for a ride. I have to think." She opened the door with trembling fingers. Somehow, she managed to walk on legs of rubber to the car, get in, and back out of the driveway.

It was a short way to the beach, but Julie wanted to be alone. She drove toward the resting place of the *Sea Queen.* This wind-blown stretch of beach was usually vacant, and today was no exception. Parking the car, she climbed out and walked to the edge of the cliff.

The once proud queen of the sea lay helplessly in the raging surf as if waiting for Julie to return. She located a grassy spot on the brink of the cliff and sat down. "Hello, Queen," Julie spoke to the rusting skeleton. "What does it feel like to be shipwrecked?" Unwelcome tears hindered Julie's vision. She wiped her eyes. "Well, you're not alone." She looked up and watched as soft, pastel clouds formed strange shapes against the blue backdrop of the sky. "What am I going to do now?" She looked at the silent ship. "Sink or...what? It's obvious," Julie said grimly, "Gary isn't really repentant at all. He just wants me to forgive and forget like nothing ever happened. It's just not that easy! Things have got to change." She bit her lip and closed her eyes. "It won't work if he doesn't really love me. What's to keep him from doing this again?"

A gust of wind suddenly swept up the bluff, scattering and rattling the tough grass. Seagulls cried out to one another as they swooped low over the surf, hunting for delicacies from the salty brine. Julie stood to her feet, brushed off her jeans and took one last, long look at her silent friend. "You know, I know," she said as she turned toward the car, "and best of all, God knows."

# 13

# ALONE IN THE NIGHT

*I watch, and am as a sparrow alone*
*upon the house top. - Psalm 102:7*

The early morning sun glistened brightly on the long expanse of shallow waves which overlapped one another in their race up the sloping shoreline. The minus tide brought with it a sense of peace and tranquility. The giant swells of the Pacific appeared unusually docile as they cascaded in foams of white far out at sea. Gulls floated lazily on unseen currents of air and communicated with one another in their own peculiar language.

Julie, standing barefoot in ankle-deep water, closed her eyes and tilted back her head. The warm rays of the golden sun caressed her uplifted face. She tried to consciously absorb its warmth, concentrating solely on those sensations which affected her five senses. The taste of salt; the touch of the gentle breeze as it tugged playfully with her hair; the smell of sunbaked seaweed left carelessly behind by the retreating tide; the sounds of the untamed and mysterious sea with its countless forms of dependent life; and the dazzling sight of crashing surf, each droplet of water a world in itself, bursting with rainbow colors of light and beauty.

Julie opened her eyes and took a deep breath. The sky overhead resembled a gigantic pearl, resplendent with opalescent bands of indescribable color. She laughed in appreciation to the Creator of the Universe. Her expression of worship was borne on the wings of the wind while the thundering surf applauded with a mixture of joy and power.

For Julie, time alone with God was the difference between life and death, sanity and insanity; especially at this crucial hour in her life. She knew she would be as shipwrecked as the *Sea Queen* without the Lord's presence, direction, and help.

"Well, Lord," Julie spoke to her Friend, "I've failed again. Made the wrong decision. Ruth had warned me he was a womanizer, but I wouldn't listen. I should've realized it wouldn't work. But I do love him." The tears that formed pools in her eyes, silently escaped, cascading in miniature rivers that dripped from Julie's face into the sea. Somehow it all seemed strangely symbolic. Everything eventually returned to its source.

Her mind replayed how the Holy Spirit had revealed Gary's affairs without leaving a trace of sordid detail. It was one of the strangest things that had ever happened to Julie. She recalled how she had approached Gary with confidence, how he had admitted to it and asked for forgiveness. Yet he had done it all so mechanically. It was as if he were a robot and she some invader from outer space, trespassing on his turf. There had been no genuine, true repentance on his part. She had thought it all through dozens of times, trying to understand what had gone wrong, what she needed to know about herself. Julie was prone to feel guilty for no reason at all, and she wanted to know the truth. The day after he was confronted, Gary had packed most of his personal belongings and driven away.

Now he was gone, leaving her in a nightmarish limbo of loneliness and confusion. Without the promises in God's Word, Julie knew she would not survive. Even so, she felt herself fighting to escape from the suffocating feeling of unreality, of being suspended in time and space. She vacillated between the relief of knowing it was finally over and sheer panic at the thought of the future. She knew her meager earnings as an artist in this small town would never sustain her. And the thought of returning to the busy, smoggy metropolis of Portland, trying to land an eight to five job just so she could live there in some apartment...well, it was just unthinkable.

"Lord," Julie walked up the sandy incline, found a suitable piece of driftwood and sat on it. "I've got to have some guidance. You know I want to serve You. Please show me what to do and how to go about it."

Julie knew by the example of Jesus what true ministry was. It was being a servant, showing genuine love, sharing, helping, witnessing, giving, and discipling one-on-one. But, in much the same way as the ocean has invisible undercurrents, so Julie had a stirring deep within her spirit. She was called to be an evangelist. A trace of a smile formed on her lips. Funny, thinking about herself being an evangelist. She used to poke fun at such a thought, telling herself and others that women should stay at home and bake cookies.

Little streams of sand collected around her toes and then blew away as if searching for a more stable resting place. Julie lifted her eyes to scan the endless expanse of beach. Great rows of sand dunes cast abstract shadows against one another as the morning sun mounted higher in the pastel sky. How she loved this place! And now that the threat of losing it was becoming a reality, sorrow mingled with fear encroached upon her heart. A sensation of guilt forced its ugly way into her mind. Had she not taken all this beauty for granted, thinking she would always be here to enjoy it whenever she wished? Now, Julie realized with a pang of regret, she had gone the way of most people. She had unknowingly, over a period of time, allowed her life to become caught up with nonessentials.

Julie forced herself to turn toward home. *If only Rose would call! She would know what to do!* Rose didn't own a cell phone, and her daughter didn't have a telephone either, so the thought of not being able to call her for fellowship and prayer added to Julie's mounting frustration. *At least I have Patsy*, she thought. *But Patsy is so tied up with her job, Daniel, and kids.*

Suddenly the realization that she was suspended between the world of the "marrieds" and the "singles" crashed against her mind. It was a strange world, a place for misfits and social outcasts. *At least that's how the church treats them,* Julie thought, *especially if they happen to be divorced women!*

Wiping the sand from her feet, Julie slid behind the wheel of her trustworthy car. She slipped on her shoes, praying at the same time. "Please, Lord, help this old car to last forever. You know I can't afford a new one!"

Julie's heart suddenly skipped a beat. It was Gary, driving toward their house! She switched on the ignition, stomped on the gas, and followed his pickup down the road and into their driveway. Gary jumped out of the truck, tugged on his baggy jeans, and walked toward Julie.

"Hi! Thought we could talk." His tone was friendly, and Julie warned herself to be cautious while at the same time fighting a powerful urge to throw herself into his arms and forget everything that had previously transpired. She waited for him to begin. "I, uh, been to the beach?"

Julie suddenly felt a surge of hot anger. How could he do this to her? How could he assume she would just forget his philandering? "Yes," she said tersely, "I've been to the beach." She waited. Whatever did he want?

"Well, I came for my rifle and a couple of things my mother gave me. I forgot them Monday." He continued to stare at her. His eyes were questioning. Perhaps he wanted to say something else, but couldn't find the courage to express it.

"Gary," Julie's voice sounded strange to her, as if it belonged to someone else. "Gary, what are you going to do?"

He dropped his gaze. "Well, that's up to you, isn't it?" Julie sucked in her breath. It seemed all the responsibility was falling on her shoulders. Before she could respond, he tipped his head and growled a second question, "Are you sure God told you?".

"Yes, Gary, God told me. He knows everything about you."

Gary scratched his head. "I always figured you kinda knew every time I did it."

Julie felt a tight knot form in the pit of her stomach. "*Every time you* did it?"

Suddenly Gary changed the course of the conversation. "Julie, I mean, it happened once." He turned his eyes toward her. They had taken on a blank look resembling a medium in a trance. "Julie, will you please forgive me?"

Julie knew her husband's tactics. It had been this way before, the false humility, the game of sorry, only to have him repeat his actions down the line. She heard herself say, "Yes, Gary, I told you I forgive you." She got out of the car and slammed the door. "Christ forgave me, and I do forgive you. But," she hastily added, putting up her hand as if to halt traffic when he took a step toward her, "you must promise me you will never do it again."

Gary looked thunderstruck. Julie was amazed at his reaction to her request. She surmised that he believed she was some weak little religious wimp who must forgive and forget every time he decided to play the field.

"Whaaaaat! Come on, Julie! I can't promise you that!" Anger registered on his masculine face. He clenched his teeth and fists simultaneously.

"Then get your stuff and leave." Julie turned toward the house. Her heart was pounding in her ears. Had she done the right thing?

As Gary gathered his belongings, the telephone rang. Julie's heart raced. Who could it be? One of Gary's girlfriends? Patsy? Could it possibly be Rose?

"Hello?" Julie was breathless.

"Hi Julie. How are you doing? I just had this sudden urge to call you!" Rose's warm voice flowed over the long distance between them. Comfort and joy wrapped around Julie's hammering heart. "Rose! Oh, am I ever glad to hear your voice! Where are you? What's happening?"

"I can't talk long, Julie, but I'm okay, except I miss you terribly. I haven't slept good on Donna's couch. And, I haven't been able to work on the manuscript, either. I just wondered how you are."

"Oh, Rose. It's so hard," Julie lowered her voice hoping Gary wouldn't overhear. "I don't want to be alone, especially at night. And, I just don't have a clue right now what the Lord wants me to do. I just want to be free of all this so I can serve Him."

Julie could hear Rose's breath on the other end of the phone. "Julie, listen to me. I've been praying and thinking. I really need your help. I can't finish the book, or minister, without you! After all, Jesus sent His disciples out in twos."

"Really? Oh, thank God. When will you be back up here?" Julie's voice vibrated with joy and relief.

"Well, I better wait for a while, Julie. If I come up there right now, I know I'll get blamed for your problems with Gary. You know how people are!" She paused, then continued, "Listen, it's almost one hundred degrees in this phone booth. And I have to go. Just know that I love and miss you a lot. Please give my love to Patsy. I'll write, honest! Bye."

Julie slowly replaced the receiver. She walked to the window and noticed Gary's truck was gone. He had slipped out the door and driven away while Julie spoke with Rose.

Silence descended on the Danza home as loneliness held Julie in its melancholy embrace. Then the darkness of night blanketed the terrain, bringing with it agonizing hours of uncertainty and depression.

# 14

# REUNION AND RUIN

*The sacrifices of God are a broken spirit: a broken and a contrite heart, O God, thou wilt not despise. - Psalm 51:17*

Time, like an invisible army, relentlessly marched on. Each day seemed to represent another soldier passing by in orderly procession.

Gary and Julie had been separated for three months. He made the house payments and picked up the other bills, but Julie knew once the divorce settlement was final, she would be on her own. There would be no steady income, no health insurance, no benefits. Occasionally this harsh truth pierced through her mind and heart like a razor-sharp arrow, sending her thoughts reeling. Fear slammed against her causing her to press harder into the Lord. Many times, in Julie's life she had sat in church and vowed she was willing to live by faith, but the true meaning of that statement had not been fully realized until now. Faith, she was discovering, meant she couldn't see anything in front of her. It meant there was no one to lean on, including herself, and no tangible security.

Julie had always felt a sense of safety within the body of Christ. Often, when in church, she would scan the people and gain a feeling of well-being. *Surely*, she thought in the back of her mind, *these good Christian people would help me if I ever became down and out.* Now that she was alone and heading for shaky ground, the shocking truth of how wrong her assumption was crashed down around her. No one had even called from the church to see how Julie was, except Mary, the one who had discipled her. And Mary only called to admonish her to stay with her husband regardless of his adulterous behavior and practice more spiritual warfare.

"If you want him to come around," Mary had stated matter-of-factly, "then you better bind the devil and pray harder."

Suddenly it dawned on Julie how cruel, unyielding, and unmerciful legalism could be. She had fasted and prayed, prayed and fasted; yet, Gary's responses were a matter of his own choices. God gave everyone freedom of choice, and if God wouldn't cross the line and force Gary to be a loving, faithful husband, then how could she be expected to do it?

*It's all so unfair,* her melancholy thoughts concluded. *It all boils down to the fact I'm a woman! Women seem to somehow always get the blame for divorce; even by other women! The whole church seems to be ignoring this situation because people are all caught up in their own lives and problems. And, besides,* she thought angrily, *he always appears to be the "good guy" because he's the one who writes checks to the church and I don't.*

Julie occupied her time sorting through her belongings in preparation for the upcoming lifestyle change. Some things she gave away and some she sold at garage sales. She also doubled her efforts to recruit new students for her art classes. There, too, she discovered the fickleness of people. Sometimes they showed up and sometimes they didn't. It was all very frustrating for her.

But the greatest blow of all was Catherine's attitude. Once she knew Gary and Julie were separated, she began chiding Julie about her role as a good wife. She went so far as to accuse Julie of being "frigid" and that, she concluded, was the cause of Gary's behavior. Catherine also informed Julie that she had called Julie's dad who lived with his wife in Washington and filled him in on the situation. Julie guessed she also told him his daughter was going down the tube.

Julie was livid. Little did her mother know! Try as she might, she couldn't convince her mother that she wasn't the culprit, that she wanted to be married, that she didn't want to launch out as a divorced woman, but Gary wouldn't promise he would remain faithful. Hurt and frustrated, Julie began withdrawing from everyone except Patsy and a few of her other close friends.

Rose began calling and writing on a regular basis which was a mixed blessing to Julie. On the one hand, hearing from Rose brought her perspective, comfort and cheer; on the other hand, not being able to be with her in ministry caused frustration, loneliness, and hopelessness.

Finally, the day came when Julie and Gary were legally divorced. She was amazed at his compliant attitude when it came to the house and the furnishings. Julie concluded guilt must be a major factor where he was concerned.

She left the courthouse alone, feeling shaken and dazed. The skies were heavy and overcast. The wind began buffeting the small community and thunder rumbled overhead. Julie stiffly got into her car and stared at her hands as they gripped the steering wheel. The gold wedding band was still on her finger. For some reason, Julie had not wanted to remove it. But now she knew it was officially over. She was a divorce statistic. With trembling hands, she slowly removed the symbol of love and put it in her purse. Choking back tears, she drove to the Cozy Cove Café.

"Julie! How are you doing?" Patsy's cheerful greeting made Julie smile.

"It's over, Patsy." Julie said softly.

"Oh, Julie. I'm so sorry." She led her friend to a private booth and put her hand gently on her arm in a gesture of sympathy.

"Look, I've quite a full load today, but I'll get you some tea. Can I get you anything else?"

Julie shook her head. "No thanks. I only have a few minutes. The realtor is showing the house today. It'll probably sell since these same people have been there three times already."

"Where are you going to live?" Patsy asked, startled.

"I don't know. But I'm confident the Lord will take care of me."

"Hey, I've got an idea! Oh, I'll be right back. I have to pour coffee." Patsy whirled and was gone for a full six minutes. She returned with Julie's tea and a toasted bagel. "Here," she said, "on me. You've got to eat something! Listen, Julie, Daniel and I have that trailer we rent out, you know, the one he had moved out to the property he inherited. It's not much, but it's empty right now. Why don't you move in there?"

Julie's pale face brightened. "Oh, Patsy, what a great idea! I'll pray about it and get back to you."

Later that day the Danza home sold. Julie began packing in earnest. She hadn't realized how much stuff she had until now. It was going to be a major headache, sorting through her last-minute possessions. She stood in the center of her living room, dazed.

Ring, ring, ring. The phone jarred Julie into action. Picking up the receiver, she heard a familiar voice on the other end. "Guess what! I'm flying up to Portland in three days. Can you pick me up?"

"Rose! You're kidding! No, you're not. Of course not. Give me the flight and the time and I'll be there with bells on."

Julie's heart began to sing. God wasn't going to leave her all alone after all!

* * *

Patsy took the day off and accompanied Julie to the airport to pick up Rose. They chatted excitedly all the way to the airport. "I'm so glad you decided to move into the trailer," Patsy grinned. "There's plenty of room for both you and Rose."

Julie nodded. *At least I have enough money from the divorce to support us for a while*, she thought. *But then what?*

"Do you think you and Rose will minister together?" Patsy asked and added without waiting for an answer, "I suppose that means you'll be traveling a lot."

"Whoa, Patsy!" Julie laughed. "Wait a minute! I'm not sure what's going to happen until Rose gets here."

Patsy changed the conversation to Gary. "Guess what? I saw Gary the other day."

Julie shot her a quick look. "Oh, where? In the café?"

"We-I-I," Patsy drawled, "Actually in two places. I saw him in the café all right and on the beach, too. Both times he was with a different woman."

"That figures," Julie said. "He has quite a track record. I found out not too long ago that he had made passes at some of my art students. He even made a pass at Ruth once." She sighed. "I really trusted Gary. I never suspected anything. Blind as a bat, as they say." She slowed the car and turned off the highway. "Here we are. The Portland airport!"

They arrived with a scant ten minutes to spare. Rose was one of the last passengers to leave the plane, and as she walked through the entry both Patsy and Julie flew in her direction at once. "Hey, girls!" she smiled broadly. "It's been a long time no see!"

The reunited trio located a nearby restaurant and after lunch happily drove back to Dayport. Julie thought about making a quick visit to Catherine's, but knowing her mother's frame of mind decided against it.

The next few days were busy ones as Rose helped Julie dispose of most of her belongings. When Julie became confused about what to keep and what to part with, Rose gently chided her about attachments to worldly things; especially things which weren't really important.

Soon the extra sets of China, antiques, knickknacks, appliances, furniture, and other items were sold. The day came when Julie and Rose moved into the McCall's trailer.

It was a difficult adjustment for Julie. Moving from a new three-bedroom, two-bathroom home with a modern kitchen, complete with top-of-the-line appliances, into a rather musty single-wide trailer with little room for furniture or storage was depressing to her. The refrigerator was badly mildewed, and try as they might, they were unsuccessful in fully eradicating it.

Rose, however, found the setting to her liking. *She's happy,* Julie thought to herself, *because she doesn't have a bunch of stuff to worry about.*

Julie and Rose worked on the manuscript and visited local churches in an attempt to secure evangelistic meetings. Much to Julie's chagrin, nothing opened up. She began to see how difficult it was to secure dates in churches for ministry. "Rose," she asked one evening as they watched the splendor of an orange and red sunset, "how did Barbara get so many meetings lined up? I mean, she went at it for years and traveled all the time."

Rose patiently explained to Julie that these things took time and that Barbara had been at it for many years. She knew plenty of Christians who helped her set up meetings. It was just a matter of time and prayer. Julie, however, gained little comfort from the knowledge that these things took a lot of time. Money was not coming in as fast as it was going out. Besides, Rose was becoming restless and homesick for Arizona. She spoke frequently about going there and how much easier it would be to set up meetings. She frequently mentioned that her children could help. Not only that, but the dampness and long, overcast days on the coast were not much to her liking.

The art classes were a thing of the past now that Julie had no room in which to teach. But one day she received a phone call from Nancy, one of her old students. "Julie," she said hurriedly, "would you like to buy my little motor home?"

"What?" Julie gasped. "I thought you said you'd never sell it!"

"We're moving back east," her friend explained, "and my husband said we should sell it and purchase a bigger one."

Julie's mind was whirling. Perhaps this was an answer from the Lord. Not only would she and Rose have a means by which to travel and have their own place to stay, but it would be a small investment for her from the money she received from the house. But how much?

"It's only $6,000, Julie," Nancy said, "and that's half what it's worth."

"Sold!" Julie exclaimed triumphantly.

Within a month Julie had sold the remainder of her furniture and possessions. The faithful Oldsmobile was stored in Ruth's yard. Julie didn't want to spend a lot of time at Ruth's, and the strained visit was short. It was obvious that Ruth would never accept Rose.

Then Julie and Rose bid a tearful farewell to Patsy with the promise of returning in the summer months. Perhaps by then Patsy would be able to secure some ministry work for them.

Julie and Rose had one more duty to attend to before leaving for Arizona, and that was to say "good-bye" to Julie's mother. The trip to Portland passed quickly. Julie took a deep breath as they pulled up in front of Catherine's charming home. Catherine herself stood on the immaculately manicured lawn. Masses of brightly colored blossoms bordered the picturesque setting. Several hanging baskets, filled to overflowing with lush blooms, swung gently in the slight breeze.

Catherine's carefully tended environment generally provided a source of comfort to her. But today nothing could soothe the stabbing pain in her heart. Tears escaped from tortured eyes and flowed down her rosy cheeks uncontrollably.

"Mom, don't..." Julie had rarely seen her mother in such distress. "It'll be okay. I'll write to you often." Julie took her mother in her arms and gave her a hug. "I love you, Mom. Good-bye."

Catherine's face seemed to crumble into a million pieces, but she continued to stand in the same position, waving her final farewell to Julie and Rose. Her opinion of Rose had not softened in the slightest. In her mind, Rose caused a divorce between her daughter and Gary. She was instrumental in helping Julie sell nearly everything she had. Her daughter's new home in Dayport was gone; the beautiful maple furniture and all the lovely furnishings, gone. Julie had even sold her antiques and custom designed diamond ring. No, as far as Catherine was concerned, Rose was to blame for everything. She could not understand her daughter. Julie had always attended Sunday School and church. She wanted to be a missionary for most of her life. But to sell it all and step out into the unknown with someone she barely knew?

She shook her head and turned toward the house. Absorbed in her musings she failed to notice the antics of two bright hummingbirds darting and zigzagging between the purple, crimson and pink blossoms. Her shoulders, usually erect and straight, were slightly stooped. Julie was her only child. How excruciating it was to watch your daughter throw it all away. How would she survive in Phoenix? Julie had never lived that far from Catherine before. Even though they had their disagreements, living thousands of miles apart was unthinkable!

Catherine walked into the small kitchen, opened the well-stocked refrigerator, found the pitcher of lemonade and poured the tangy liquid over a glass of ice. "Well," she said to no one but herself and the small, blonde Pomeranian dancing at her feet, "She's a big girl now. If she wants to be a fool, that's up to her."

Meanwhile, Julie tried to dowse the hot flame of anguish threatening to consume her soul. How endless and deep was her love for her mother! She was nearly numb with sorrow. She tightened her grip on the steering wheel.

"Julie," Rose turned toward her. Her eyes were full of understanding, sympathy, and compassion. "I know it's hard, Julie. But following Christ isn't always easy. He never said it was going to be fun all the time. You can stay here if you don't want to go."

"Are you kidding? Don't say that! I've waited for years for this opportunity to serve God. If I didn't believe in His call on your life, and my own desire to be His servant, I wouldn't have purchased this motor home with the divorce money. And," Julie's eyes sparkled, "You are truly a rose, a sweet fragrance to both God and me."

Rose leaned back against the tan and ivory upholstered seat and closed her eyes. "Julie, I," she hesitated, then continued in a hushed and somber tone, "remember, roses have thorns."

# 15

# FREE AT LAST!

*Lead me, O Lord, in thy righteousness . . .*
*make thy way straight before my face. - Psalm 5:8*

The small motor home was easy to drive, and Julie's tight muscles began to relax. She silently praised the Lord for all His kindness and mercy. Everything was going to work out fine, she was certain of it.

"It sure was the hand of God bringing this motor home along like He did!" Rose said happily. "And to think it only cost half of what it's really worth!"

"I know! It's so exciting to think about how the Lord directs our steps. But," she added, "it sure was a horrible battle getting through the past few months. Gary pretended to be a such good Christian the whole time. I heard he even took one of his girlfriends to church before the divorce was final! And nobody said a word to him about it!" She grimaced slightly and continued, "But what really hurt me the most was what Ruth and her cousin, April, did to me."

Rose looked at Julie. "I'm so sorry you had to go through that experience by yourself. I just couldn't leave the kids at that time to get back up here. Besides, it just wouldn't look good for me to be living with you and Gary." She lapsed into silence.

95

Julie's mind raced backwards to that horrible day when Ruth and April had come for a visit upon hearing the news of Gary and Julie's imminent divorce. They wrote their names on small scraps of paper and went through her house, affixing their names on lamps, tables, chairs, and other items which they claimed as their own in the event Julie had to sell them. Julie felt as if her bones had been picked clean by two vultures before she was pronounced fully dead. It gave her an odd sensation which she never could quite describe. She watched them back out of the driveway, chattering happily to each other, and then disappear as they turned the corner at the end of her street. Julie had turned away from the window, walked straight to her bedroom and plopped on the waterbed, laughing and crying all at the same time.

"Are you alright?" Rose's question jarred Julie back to the present.

"Yeah, I'm okay; just thinking. It may take time, but I really do want to follow the Lord, and I know what it means to take up my cross. I have to let go of everything and not hang on to the things of this world like I have in the past." She sighed, then added, "I couldn't have made it without you, Rose. I'm so glad you helped me with my perspective about life. There were days when I thought I'd lose my mind. I recall the evening I stood alone in my hallway. Gary had been gone for a few weeks. Suddenly, my mind went blank. I had absolutely no feelings one way or the other. I came that close to becoming a zombie! I reminded myself of a tree, you know, alive but unable to function as a normal human being."

Julie glanced at Rose. Her friend was listening intently. Julie added thoughtfully, "There will never be another man in my life! I don't ever want to go through this again!"

"Believe me, Julie," Rose said with conviction, "Jesus makes the best husband. I know. And," her voice became tinged with grief, "I can certainly relate to betrayal after what Barbara Weston put me through. I worked so hard for her, trying to help her in her ministry. But," she quickly added, "I've forgiven her and I'll always love and pray for her."

There was much Julie didn't understand. Barbara Weston was a mystery to her. It was beyond her mental ability at this time to try and understand how such a woman of God could selfishly take off for Africa and leave her faithful co-laborer with nothing. *But, then, God's ways certainly are higher than our ways,* she thought. *We can't always understand why He does what He does. But I'm certain if the Lord hadn't sent Rose into my life at this time, I would have been driven to total insanity by this situation with Gary.*

Julie sucked in the fresh air blowing through the open window. It felt refreshing against her face. She smiled at Rose, "I'm glad we got through the 'good-byes' okay up there in Portland, but I'll sure miss Patsy and Daniel like crazy." Rose nodded in agreement. Patsy and Daniel had become very close to Rose and often sent her money.

A burst of wind pulled at Julie's wavy hair, flinging it wildly in the air. A shiver of exhilaration flooded her body. "Hallelujah!" she shouted above the roar of the engine. "Here we go! Free at last!"

# 16

# FAREWELL FOREST, HELLO DESERTS

*I am a stranger in the earth:*
*hide not thy commandments from me. - Psalm 119:19*

Julie switched the windshield wipers to high and squinted against the glare of approaching headlights. "Whew!" What a storm! I can barely see to drive. Let's stop at the next rest area, okay?"

Rose yawned and stretched out her legs. "That's a good idea. We need to be careful, though."

Julie knew by Rose's tone she wasn't kidding. For the past two days their conversations had alternated between serious discussions concerning God and His word to hilarity beyond anything Julie had yet experienced. She felt a genuine friendship for Rose growing deeper with each passing day. "What do you mean?" Julie respected the experience Rose had gained while traveling with Barbara.

"Oh, it's just not safe at the rest areas anymore. Barbara and I had some real hairy things happen to us when we traveled together." Rose lapsed into silence. Julie knew she was thinking about Barbara and broke in quickly. "Well, what kinds of things *do* happen at those places?"

Rose gave a small chuckle. "Julie, you really have been protected a lot, I can tell. Well, one time a couple of men approached us when we pulled into the parking area. They pretended to be having some sort of problem with their truck and wanted us to take them down the highway. It's a good thing the door was locked and I had the motor running because when I declined, they tried to jerk the door open."

Julie's pulse quickened. Yes, she had been protected most of her life. This was the first time she had left friends and family to start a new life. She repeatedly told herself to have faith in God and grow up. But pain of divorce, the apparent betrayal of her church, the sorrow in Catherine's eyes, and the nagging fear of the future in an unfamiliar place weighed heavily on Julie's heart. Already the expense of traveling nibbled away at Julie's resources like a ravenous rat nibbles on a hunk of cheese. She knew she would need to depend on God like never before.

"Julie, are you all right?" Rose looked intensely at her friend.

"Oh, yes, I'm fine. Just tired, that's all. What were you saying?"

Rose leaned back against the headrest. "The men who tried to get into our car were sure surprised when I shoved it in reverse and hit the gas."

"Here we are. Rest area!" Julie pulled the motor home into a well-lit space and turned off the engine. "We'll make sure everything is locked and stick together." She stretched and yawned. "I am so exhausted! I can't wait to get to bed."

But late into the night Julie lay awake. The intensity of the storm lessened, but continued to express itself with sporadic splatters of rain. Julie listened as a short squall pelted the metal roof. By tomorrow night they should be in Arizona. Then they would have to find a park for the motor home and work out an itinerary for Rose. *In the meantime,* Julie thought, *I'll have to try and work up an art class to bring in some income. But, on the other hand, if Rose and I are going to minister on the road, I can't get tied down to a permanent job.* Images of traveling with Rose floated through Julie's weary mind, only to be overshadowed by visions of the demanding job of teaching painting classes.

"Oh, Lord, please help me!" Julie prayed silently. "I need help if I am to be Your faithful servant. I know to be the greatest in the kingdom is to be a servant. Help me to serve Your servant, Rose. I need to know what to do." Julie finally relaxed and fell into a deep sleep.

The following day the scenery decidedly changed. Julie was glad it was Rose's turn to drive. She noticed everything and tried to commit to memory the exotic shapes of desert rocks, plant life, majestic clouds, colors, and compositions for future use as subject for paintings.

Rose knew her way through the desert terrain well and fought the temptation to accelerate over the legal limit. She threw back her head and laughed. "Oh, Julie! Just feel that wonderful, warm desert air! No overcast skies out here!"

Julie smiled. Yes, it would be all right. All she had to do was take one day at a time. Somehow it would work out. "Rose, where do we start? I mean, do we contact pastors of churches, or what?"

Rose's face took on that special glow Julie loved to see. There was something unexplainable about Rose when she looked this way that stirred Julie's spirit. "Julie," Rose's voice sounded almost transformed. Julie felt as if she was in the presence of an angel. "God knows where He wants us. He will open the doors at the right time. Don't worry, my friend."

Julie felt a twinge of guilt. She definitely had a lot to learn about faith. The brilliant blue canopy of sky, the dazzling brightness and warmth of the desert sun temporarily relieved Julie's mounting anxiety.

But soon darkness swiftly descended like a thick, black shroud over the empty stretches of barren wasteland. Occasionally, small nocturnal animals could be seen, caught by the beam of the headlights, only to quickly scurry to safety as the motor home swished past.

Rose hummed a hymn to herself, obviously content to be nearing her children. Julie, however, felt tension mounting in her body. Her neck and back ached, and she longed to soak in a hot tub.

Suddenly lights appeared. Julie leaned forward and peered through the bug splattered windshield. Thousands of lights greeted her astonished eyes.

"Hallelujah! We're getting close! There it is, Phoenix!" Rose made no effort to conceal her joy. But for Julie, it was a moment of dread. In the vast desert darkness, the metropolis appeared to stretch from one edge of the world to the other.

"Yeah," she responded quietly. Julie was glad Rose couldn't see her face in the dimly lit cab. She turned and stared out the window. Tears streamed unchecked down her face and fear gripped her heart, threatening to squeeze every ounce of strength from her body. "Oh, God," her mind fought against the paralyzing grip of sheer panic, "Lord, I need You. You know I don't know a living soul in that huge place, except Rose. I'm so scared! What am I going to do? Please speak to me!"

Julie closed her eyes and tried to concentrate on hearing the voice of the Spirit. But, other than the rhythmic drone of the engine, the only sound to greet Julie's ears was Rose, softly humming "Amazing Grace."

# 17

# FROM FEAR TO FAIRYTALES

*In thee, O Lord, do I put my trust:*
*let me never be put to confusion. - Psalm 71:1*

The shapely Mexican waitress deftly set salsa, chips, tortillas, and tacos on the small, round table. "I'll be right back with more Pepsi for you, senoritas!"

Donna smiled at her sister, Debbie. Donna had Rose's smile and dark, thick hair while Debbie, blonde and fair, had her mother's nose, chin and cheekbones. "I love this place. Never get tired of it." Donna's engagement ring sparkled as she reached for a chip.

Debbie pursed her full lips and a slight frown creased her flawless brow. "Donna," she began, her hazel eyes fastening on her older sister's suntanned face, "I wonder what Mom plans to do this time."

"What do you mean?" Donna's voice reflected a note of irritation. She wanted to savor every moment in her favorite Mexican restaurant and not be reminded of problems beyond her ability to control.

"Well," Debbie began cautiously, "I mean, I just wonder if she is going to have meetings around here, how long she's going to stay, and . . ." her voice trailed off. Debbie realized too late she never should have brought up the subject of their evangelist mother.

Donna stared at Debbie; her corn chip poised in mid-air. "And, what?" Her green eyes seemed to bore holes into Debbie's face.

"Well, you know. I mean, what's she gonna say about you and Ralph living together now?"

Sparks flew from Donna's eyes, resembling the miniature flecks of light escaping from her diamond ring. "Debbie, I really don't give a rip what she thinks. Besides," she added as she drug the obtrusive chip through her salsa, "I think she already has an idea Ralph is sharing my apartment. And we *are* planning to get married you know!"

The waitress returned with a pitcher of Pepsi and a container of ice cubes. "Will that be all?" Debbie nodded, "Yes, thank you."

"No, I've decided to have a beer," Donna interrupted.

Debbie pressed her lips together. It would be best if she changed the subject. But her attempts were unsuccessful. Donna, now aroused, was determined to pursue the subject to the end. "Listen, Deb, I respect Mom's religion and all that, but we're not living in the dark ages anymore. Besides," she threw back her head and laughed, "Mom loves me no matter what. You know how she is with all three of us. Now that she's back in our lives we're literally smothered to death." She took a bite out of her taco, chewed thoughtfully, swallowed and continued. "Just think of Duane. He simply can do no wrong as far as Mom's concerned. She has to know by now Rita moved in with him!"

Debbie winced. While she wasn't as committed to God as her mother, she still tried to live a moral life outwardly; especially after her affair with Sean. It had left her with not only a broken heart, but enough guilt to last the rest of her life. "I just hope Mom does all right, that's all. That Barbara Weston about destroyed her. We don't know a thing about...what's her name?"

"It's Julie. Julie Danza." Donna paused, thanked the waitress for the beer, and continued. "According to Mom, she's an artist who just got a divorce and who wants to go on the road with her." Donna waved her finger in the air as if trying to corner a stray thought. "And, Deb, by the way, try and remember what really happened. I know you were young, but it was Mom who left us and went with Barbara. Even though she blames Dad, I remember what really happened. She wanted to run off with that Barbara Weston. Nobody drug her out of the house. She just up and left."

Debbie took a bite of her tortilla. "Donna," she paused and poured Pepsi over the ice in her tall glass. She watched it fizz and bubble for a moment and then continued, "It's all confusing to me. Dad says one thing and Mom says another. She insists she didn't want to leave us, but she was forced to." She sipped the cool drink, and added thoughtfully, "Sometimes I really feel Mom should try to get a job. I know she has some physical problems because of her weight, but there must be something she could do to help herself financially. She doesn't have insurance or anything. And that old junker of hers is about to fall apart. Besides," she said dejectedly, "the rest of us have to work." Debbie watched Donna enthusiastically attack her taco. She went on, "I know she wants to travel and preach, but I worry about her running all over the countryside. And for what?"

Donna stopped chewing and pointed a fork at her younger sister. Her green eyes looked straight into Debbie's. "Look, Deb," her tone was even. "We can't do anything about it. It's her life, she is old enough to take care of herself, and we have our own lives to live. Yes, I'd love to have her here in Phoenix all the time, but ever since..." Donna's voice quavered slightly. She quickly regained control and went on, "Ever since their divorce when we were teenagers, Mom has been on the road. It's her choice. At this time, I feel it's more important to help Daddy. He's the one with tremendous health and financial problems. Mom always manages to find somebody to help her." She took a long drink of beer, dabbed at her lips with the red linen napkin and glanced at her watch. "Good grief! I have only fifteen minutes to pick up Ralph from work. He gets off early today. We have to run over to the dealer and get his truck and then clean up the apartment. Mom should be getting into town any time." She pushed back her chair and stood to her feet.

Debbie put a tip on the table, picked up her purse and looked up at her sister. "Donna, where on earth are Mom and her friend going to stay when they get here? None of us have any room to spare and now that Ralph has moved in with you . . ."

A look of exasperation swept over Donna's suntanned face. "For Pete's sake, Deb, would you drop it? Apparently, this Julie has a small RV. They'll have to put it in a park somewhere I suppose. It's against city ordinances to park RV's in people's driveways you know. I'm sure they have it figured out. Maybe Julie has a lot of dough. I dunno." She walked to the cash register, paid for both lunches and turned to Debbie. "I'll call you if I hear from Mom, okay? And if you hear from her first, you call me."

Debbie managed to smile weakly. "Thanks for the lunch, Donna. I'll let you know if I hear anything."

Meanwhile, Rose and Julie walked stiffly to the telephone booth near the small office of the RV park. "Boy, am I ever exhausted from such a long trip," Julie yawned. "We got in pretty late last night. And then to think we nearly didn't get a place to park! God sure is good to give us the last space here." She looked around the crowded RV park. Most of the guests were retirees. They openly stared at the two women and whispered to each other. It was obvious to Julie that she and Rose were already the subject of gossip.

Julie waited as Rose dialed Donna's number. She listened as she gave a short message to the answering machine. Rose hung up the receiver and wiped perspiration from her brow with the back of her hand. "Hey, partner," she said with a grin. "Let's go get some iced tea and talk about what we'd like to do."

Julie was glad when they finally settled into a comfortable booth in a nearby café. As with most businesses in Phoenix, it was air conditioned. Even though it was early spring, temperatures already far exceeded the range Julie was accustomed to.

After placing their order, Rose's gaze rested on Julie's tired face. "Julie," her voice was barely audible. "I can't tell you how happy I am God allowed us to be together. We are going to have some wonderful and exciting times."

Julie visibly relaxed. The tension and fear of the night before melted like ice left exposed to the intense heat of the desert sun. As they sipped the cold beverage and shared their hearts' desires to serve the Lord, Julie's tortured mind began to envision future ministry with Rose. The evangelist outlined several avenues of ministry she hoped to pursue. There would be the book, and then perhaps another one or two. Halls could be rented, flyers and posters made up, seminars offered, women's retreats attended, and Bible studies made available.

Julie's mind spun with joy. At last, at long last her lifelong dream was about to come true. Or was it?

# 18

# FURNACE OF FIRE

*... if I make my bed in hell, behold,*
*thou art there. - Psalm 139:8b*

The timid rap on the RV door was barely audible, but Rose quickly jumped to her feet. "They're here!" she exclaimed triumphantly. She gingerly turned the handle and swung the door open. Julie looked up and saw three young women and two young men peering into the crowded space. "Donna, Debbie, Duane!" Rose's voice rang with joy. "Oh, I'm so happy to see you! Hello Ralph and Rita. How are you?" She stepped out of the narrow opening, embracing each one in turn.

Suddenly Julie felt out of place and alone. She sat quietly on the narrow couch, trying to look casual. She waited through a long and uncomfortable silence as Rose, now reunited with her daughters, son and their partners, chatted excitedly. Finally, she opened the door and motioned for Julie to join them. It was obvious the small RV couldn't handle such a crowd.

Julie slowly rose, and self-consciously stepped outside. Introductions were made and Julie stood silently observing the animated conversations taking place between the little crowd. Rose, never once glancing in Julie's direction, was obviously fully absorbed in her own world. Occasionally one or more of the young people looked over at Julie questioningly.

*It seems so strange,* Julie thought, *that such an upright, godly woman as Rose would have such worldly children.* She could tell by their dress and demeanor that none of them shared Rose's enthusiasm for the ministry.

Finally, the little reunion ended, the visitors hugged Rose good-bye, and they left. Julie and Rose re-entered their cramped living quarters. Julie put the kettle on the gas stove. She felt like a good stiff cup of tea. For some reason she was strangely disturbed and somewhat depressed.

"Well," Rose sighed as she sat down at the little table. "Aren't they precious? I love them so very much." She searched Julie's drawn face. "I might just as well tell you," she said suddenly, "that my children aren't exactly living what would be an acceptable lifestyle as far as the church may be concerned, but," there was a warning note in her voice, "they all know the truth and have accepted Christ in the past. I just love and accept them where they are and try not to preach at them."

Confusion swept over Julie followed by creeping twinges of guilt. Perhaps she was too judgmental. After all, she had no business casting the first stone. She stared at the teakettle as if willing it to boil.

"Well, my friend," Rose broke the silence amiably, "after your tea, let's go out for a walk. The Arizona nights are so wonderful and balmy. We can look at the stars."

* * *

The cool pine forests of the Pacific Northwest seemed like an elusive and strangely dim memory for Julie. Her tired mind and aching, swollen body felt sluggish in the searing summer heat. Even the faintest effort to mentally picture the lush greenery of her home state was an effort.

Sometimes, when temperatures soared into the hundreds, Julie would close her eyes and try to recapture memories of leisurely walks on vacated sweeping expanses of beach. She imagined herself moving through swirling wisps of cold, wet fog, while the still and mysterious sea played hide and seek through the damp, gray curtain.

Julie had tried in vain to prepare herself for the onslaught of summer. Since she and Rose's arrival several months previously, each day registered the inevitable ascendancy of summer's blistering temperatures. The air conditioning unit on their small motor home proved to be inadequate, and that, plus the overcrowded living conditions, forced the two friends to locate a place to rent.

They found a small home in a moderately decent neighborhood. Donna and Debbie loaned them a few pieces of furniture and other household necessities. Unfortunately, the house was cooled with a swamp cooler rather than an air conditioner. It proved to be inefficient and did little to relieve the suffocating heat.

Rose seemed to be fairly content, however, and it was obvious to Julie that being close to her family brought a measure of fulfillment which was lacking when traveling elsewhere. She continued to labor over the manuscript, typing and retyping her testimony. Julie began to become impatient with the long, drawn-out process, but when Rose practiced solos for future meetings, Julie momentarily cast off her anxieties, releasing her spirit to soar in ecstasy with every note.

Eventually Rose decided she needed a new laptop computer if she were to complete her book. Julie wasn't overjoyed with Rose's conclusion, but she was willing to do whatever it took to bring the laborious task to a successful conclusion. The day came to shop for a computer. Not knowing that a used computer out of the newspaper would be adequate, Julie consented to purchasing a new system with her credit. Rose's excitement did little, however, to overcome Julie's apprehension over the financial situation. Little by little she was being plunged into credit card debt she had no way of paying.

"Don't worry, Julie," Rose chided her good-naturedly. "God knows what we need, and He never fails. He'll bring in the money if we just trust Him for it."

"But, Rose! That's my name on all this stuff. I just don't believe it is God's will that we go into debt!"

Since ministry had not opened up as Julie expected, and because her money was rapidly dwindling, Julie sought every opportunity to provide income. She worked part time for a temporary job service, became involved with a home decorating company which kept her busy doing home showings at night and on weekends, and sought out art galleries. She did everything in her power to market her art talent. She managed to hold several small classes in RV parks and in two frame shops. Occasionally, Julie would be commissioned to do a portrait, which somewhat helped diminish the mounting stack of unpaid bills.

Julie was accustomed to small-town folks who exuded genuine good will and friendliness. She was unprepared, therefore, to cope with those who maintained a pose of indifference. This aloof and unfriendly demeanor of many of her art students baffled Julie. She was an outgoing and personable woman and could not relate to what she called "city snobbery."

Meanwhile, Julie knew Rose's heart ached for her children's spiritual life, but she also knew criticism on her part would not be well-received by their mother. At least Donna, and occasionally Duane, attended Bible studies in their home. All three of Rose's children treated Julie with politeness, but she sensed their reluctance to totally accept her. She often wondered what they had experienced in their young lives to cause this suspicious nature. But she knew, without a doubt, that Rose loved them obsessively.

Julie was willing to do anything, however, that God required of her to further the gospel. She worked diligently with Rose, making corrections on the manuscript and giving necessary moral support when the task became overwhelming. But this particular day Julie's resolve appeared to evaporate in the incessant desert heat. "Rose, I just can't stand it here anymore. I'm sorry, but this place is too hot. I've got to get out of here!" Julie's red hair clung to her damp face.

Rose smiled patiently. "I have a surprise for you!" She waved a piece of wrinkled paper in the air.

"What is that?" Julie failed to see how this seemingly insignificant piece of paper could relieve her distress.

Rose chuckled. "It's a note from Nolene Davis, you know, my friend in Montana." Julie's eyebrows raised questioningly. "Julie, my friend, we are going north!"

"What? How? When?" Julie jumped to her feet and clasped her hands together in excitement. Rose's face registered a strange mixture of joy and sorrow. "Nolene set up some meetings for me which start in a couple of months. She's terrific at contacting pastors and securing revival meetings." She looked out the window suddenly lost in thought. Finally, she turned to Julie and said, "We have to give the landlord notice and get our belongings in order. So," her voice softened as she noticed the look of despair in Julie's eyes, "we will have to put up with the heat for a little while yet, but at least we know we will be going out to do the Lord's work! Besides, it'll take time for you to fulfill all your art commitments, and I want to continue the Bible studies here with Donna and Duane as long as possible."

As preparations began for the long trip north, Julie's sagging spirit began to revive. She had always loved Montana, and now they would be serving God in this beautiful place. Rose decided that since the motor home was too small to tow her car, she should drive her car to Kalispell with Julie following in the small motor home. This way they would have a car to run around in once the RV was situated. "That car is really a classic," Rose told her, shaking her head sadly, "but it needs to be worked on." Julie's heart went out to Rose. She felt overwhelmed by the suffering this servant of God had experienced. Almost impulsively she agreed to restore the ailing vehicle.

Julie's excitement was dampened by the obvious unhappiness Rose exhibited whenever it came to the thought of leaving her adult children. But Julie was positively sure of one thing: Rose wanted more than anything else in the whole world to serve the Lord.

# 19

# MONTANA IN THE MORNING

*My voice shalt thou hear in the morning,*
*Lord; in the morning will I direct my prayer*
*unto thee, and will look up. - Psalm 5:3*

Julie moaned softly and tossed under the heavy quilt. Alone in the small motor home, she drifted in and out of sleep. Misty memories of the recent past haunted her dreams. Gary's face loomed before her. She saw his eyes, cold and demonic floating closer and closer. Hands reached for her throat. Julie screamed, but no sound escaped from her parted lips. Then a hatchet appeared and panic gripped her heart. Again, no sound came as she shrieked in her tortured mind. "No! No, Gary, no! Help me, somebody, Rose, somebody, help me! Jesus! Help me!"

Julie flung the quilt to the floor and sat up with a jerk. She stared blankly at the floor for a moment, trying to catch her breath. The cold, damp air wrapped around her shivering shoulders, causing her to grab at the quilt. She tried to run her fingers through the explosion of red hair that tumbled over her pale face. "Rose?" Julie's eyes swung wildly around the cluttered space. Rose was nowhere in sight. It was obvious she had never come home last night from Nolene and Hank Davis's place.

Julie sighed deeply. Ever since their arrival in Kalispell, Rose spent less and less time with her travel partner. Although she was thankful to the ever-energetic Nolene for setting up meetings, Julie felt an inexplicable prick of anxiety. She swung her legs over the edge of the rumpled bed and fumbled through a pile of clothes hoping to find clean underwear. "This is the pits!" Julie exclaimed to herself. "Oh Lord, I'm so sorry. I know I should be thankful, but..." A gust of wind rocked the small RV and huge raindrops began pelting the metal roof. Soon loud splatters gave way to a steady roar as the cloudburst vented its relentless fury.

Drip, drip, drip, drip. "No! Oh no! Please God, no!" Julie fought a tide of mounting anger and frustration as she reached in the narrow cupboard for a pot. Shoving it on the small table to catch the intruding water, she sank onto the seat and tried to calm her jangled nerves. But the chilly air quickly roused her. *Oh, yeah, I remember now,* Julie thought miserably. *The propane heater went out last night.* "Probably out of propane," she mumbled dejectedly.

The door rattled and swung open, interrupting Julie's one-way conversation. "Hey! How're ya doin'?" Rose's cheerful voice jarred Julie's frayed nerves. She climbed inside the cramped quarters and banged the door shut. Julie detected the smell of coffee and bacon and eggs clinging to Rose's jacket. "We have a leak?"

"Yes, we have a leak!" Julie answered sarcastically. Rose set her jaw and stared at Julie in disapproval. Julie looked at her and continued, "Rose, we, I, uh...this is impossible, living like this. I mean we don't have enough space to work, or live, and now that the meetings are over with and no more are scheduled, what are we going to do?"

Rose tipped her head and smiled weakly. "Julie, you don't have to live like this if you don't want to. You're free to go back to Oregon any time you want."

"Are you kidding?" Julie's eyes filled with tears. "We've been through so much together, and the book isn't finished, and..."

Rose's eyes probed Julie's tortured face. "Julie, I told you in the beginning it wasn't a 'glory trail' to serve the Lord. Now, you know the last four meetings we held here in Montana were well-received. I know the people were deeply touched."

*Well, I'm sure glad you know that,* Julie thought sardonically, *since nobody came forward for salvation or to repent at a single one of them.*

"...and," Rose concluded, "I believe God used Nolene to open doors, and if we don't panic, and we press in and pray, God will open other doors. Right now, God knows I am exhausted and need a few weeks to rest."

Julie's mouth dropped open in surprise. "Rest? But...but, I thought we'd be having continuous ministry up here. What're we going to do, and how are we going to survive financially? I don't want to take the last bit of savings I have out of the bank if we can at least book other meetings!"

Anger flashed across Rose's face. Her lips tightened into a thin line, but she said nothing. Instead, she silently stood to her feet, glanced up at the ceiling, stared at the leak and exited the motor home. The door closed with a bang.

Julie's mounting frustration, loneliness, and fear threatened to drown her in a deluge of misery. She fought for control by forcing herself into action. Standing to her feet, she maneuvered around the persistent leak and straightened the pile of clothes and other items piled on the small seat. "Okay, Lord," she said with new resolve, picking up a sweatshirt and folding it. "You said to be of good courage and then you would strengthen my heart. I don't understand how that works, but I'll begin to act as if I have courage!"

But in the back of her mind nagging doubts struggled to emerge into the mainstream of Julie's thinking much like bubbles escaping from the bottom of the ocean journey through currents and obstacles to finally explode on the surface. Rose's responses could definitely be baffling at times. Julie was aware her initial resolve and determination was rapidly eroding. Twinges of doubt and fear assailed her confused mind. *How can Rose not be concerned about our plight? We're basically stranded, Julie* told herself. *Well,* another voice echoed out of the realm of darkness, *you just lack faith, Julie. Can't you see you're not really a woman of great faith like Rose? You miss the comforts you used to have. Your heart still longs for the things of the world, just like the disobedient children of Israel. Julie, you're basically a loser.*

"Satan! I rebuke you in the Name of Jesus Christ!" Julie flung the sweatshirt across the small space. It hit the back of the seat, clinging to the plaid fabric, sleeves jauntily outstretched as if it had a personality all its own. Julie giggled. The incessant dripping had stopped and shafts of sunshine slanted through the open window. "That's enough lies! God is going to deliver us, and soon!"

# 20

# WHISTLE WITH THE WIND

*The eyes of the Lord are upon the righteous,*
*and his ears are open unto their cry. - Psalm 34:15*

"Praise the Lord! This is wonderful! A miracle! What an answer to prayer!" Julie threw back her head and laughed. Even her long red hair, gently blowing in the autumn breeze, seemed to rejoice.

Rose's eyes twinkled with merriment. She kept step with Julie as they approached the front porch of the old farmhouse. "This is exactly what we've asked the Lord for." Rose's voice reminded Julie of how she imagined an angel would sound. "The rent is so cheap! And, we can pick up what furniture we need from rummage sales in town."

Together they entered the empty structure. Cobwebs swung lazily in the corners, and the sound of a mouse scurrying for safety greeted them. Julie spotted two dead birds lying under the front room window and gasped. "Ugh!" Her eyes widened. "We certainly have a lot of work cut out for us here." Noticing Rose's eyes upon her, she quickly added cheerfully, "But, together we can do it."

The old farmhouse was situated about seven miles from Nolene and Hank's place. Every Saturday Julie and Rose drove the distance to search through yard sales with the Davis's for the bargain of the week. *Funny,* Julie told herself on one of their outings, *how my life has changed. Instead of perfectly matched* *maple furniture, I now have a 75–cent, broken-down kitchen chair, a $3.50 living room chair, and $20 sofa, not to mention 50-cent curtains!*

Six weeks after Julie and Rose had moved into the old house, it smelled fresh from scrubbing and disinfecting. The mismatched curtains hung in the windows while the assortment of yard sale bargain furniture filled the rooms. Julie's paintings completed the homey scene, and a fire sizzled and crackled in the wood stove, promising to dispel the chilly fall air.

Julie looked up from the book she was reading and glanced at her watch. "I wonder when Rose will be home," she said under her breath. She was tired from a long day in Pineville where she had arranged with the local frame and office supply shop to hold painting classes there. Once again, Julie's anxiety caused by overdue bills had forced her into action. She fought against the depression that threatened to engulf her.

*It's so terribly lonely in this big house without Rose,* Julie admitted to herself. *I hate sitting out here all by myself. God, is this where I'm really supposed to be?* As if in answer to Julie's silent musings, the wind, which only an hour ago had been frivolously tossing and teasing the orange and yellow leaves from the trees in their front yard into playing games of tag, now slammed against the weather-beaten siding in earnest. Small cracks around the old windows gave way to ghostly sounds of whistling and moaning, causing Julie to stir herself off the uncomfortable couch. She walked stiffly to the stack of split pine, selected a small log, and threw it into the hissing fire. The eager flames wrapped their golden tongues around the helpless piece of wood.

Julie was thankful for a place to live, a place which served as not only a base for their ministry, but also afforded her the luxury of an upstairs 'north light' artist's studio as well. But the initial joy she experienced was overshadowed by clouds of doubt and insecurity.

"Well," Julie said abruptly to herself as she turned toward the kitchen, "I might just as well grab the bull by the horns and think this thing through." She ran water into the teakettle and put it on the borrowed two-burner hot plate. Yes, she had a date for tea with herself and her jumbled thoughts. "It's time to figure this out, Julie Danza," she told herself.

By the time the tea was steeped and Julie was settled close to the hissing fire, her thoughts began rushing through her mind like wild horses charging through a narrow canyon. *Yes,* she factually concluded, *it is true, ever since Rose and I met Melody, a subtle change has come over Rose. Of course, Melody is a blessing because she offered the house to us for such low rent, yet...* Julie looked out the kitchen window toward the dim outline of Melody's large, Victorian house and barn silhouetted against the murky sky. A faint light could be seen emanating from the dining room window, and Julie felt a rush of frustration and anger.

"Why don't you at least call me and let me know if you're coming home to eat dinner?" It felt good to give voice to her churning emotions. "How can we serve God together if you're always parked down at Melody's? Don't you care that I'm all alone most of the time in this big old, cold house—way out here in the middle of nowhere?" Julie looked over at the wobbly, scratched table next to her and reached for a tissue. She buried her face in it.

"So, Julie," she chided herself, "since you're so smart, why is all your money gone? Why did you fix up that old car of hers instead of keeping some reserve back in the bank for tough times?" She blew her nose and leaned back in the faded chair. She lifted her eyes to the ceiling as if somehow, she could stare right through it and into heaven. "Oh God!" she moaned, "I promised to help Rose, but You must give me strength to go on and the wisdom to be able to help her finish that book!" Julie felt suddenly weak and sick to her stomach. It seemed like a century had passed since the initial work began on Rose's autobiography back in Oregon. Rose seemed to avoid the challenge of finishing the book, and when she did manage to spend a few hours on it, would only rewrite what she had previously written.

But Melody, well, there just weren't words to describe this beautiful and mysterious woman who was in her mid-forties. She lived alone and preferred it that way. Somehow, she managed to survive in spite of the alluring and baffling stories which circulated through the community about her. Some said her house was haunted and that the ghost of her dead son could be seen walking through the fields which surrounded her farm on moonlit nights. Others said she had lost a lover early in her life and that you could hear his voice calling her name when the wind blew through the stately pine trees. Julie had to admit if ever there was such a thing as a haunted house, Melody's would be it. Otherwise, all she knew for certain was that ever since they met Melody, Rose began to change.

It wasn't discernable at first, but as time went on, Rose withdrew more and more from Julie and spent long hours with Melody. It grated on Julie that Rose exerted herself to help Melody work around her farm and home, but neglected to lift the burden where Julie was concerned. Rose and Melody seemed to somehow share a common mystical experience unknown to Julie. She felt like an outsider, although when she was with them, they included her as an equal. Even in such times, however, Julie always felt as if there was an invisible wall erected to keep her out.

Sometimes Julie's loneliness, like a lasso, wrapped itself around her imagination, tugging her towards thoughts of remarriage. She imagined meeting a man like Paul, except he would have to be sold out for God. Then she would sternly reprimand herself, bringing to remembrance the teaching of the church; no more husbands, no more marriage. She was divorced.

Julie shifted her weight uncomfortably. Suddenly she exclaimed, "All right, here goes." She climbed out of the overstuffed chair and headed for the phone. She dialed Melody's number. "Hi, Melody. This is Julie. May I speak to Rose, please?" She listened to muffled sounds of conversation followed by laughter. Finally, Rose spoke into the receiver. "Yeah, what's up?"

"Well, for one thing," Julie blurted loudly, "are you coming home to eat or do I have to eat all by myself again?" She sensed Rose's displeasure. After a pause which seemed to last for hours, Rose responded in a level tone. "Julie, you are free to eat any time you want. You can come here and visit if you want. I'm busy helping Melody."

"What do you mean, you're helping Melody? We have our own ministry to work on you know. Your book isn't finished, we need to get a newsletter out, and last, but not least, don't you think we should work on an itinerary so you can fulfill the call to preach?" The momentum of her words caught Julie off guard. She waited, trembling, for Rose's reply.

"I have to go. Good-bye!" The receiver clicked sharply in Julie's ear.

A puff of frigid air escaping from the flimsy windowpane silently wrapped itself around Julie. She involuntarily shuddered under the invisible shroud as it penetrated her sweater and crawled up her skin. She wrapped her arms around her thin body and walked briskly to the small wood stove.

"No!" she whispered hoarsely as she jerked open the creaky door of the inadequate stove. She stared at the dying embers of the once glowing fire. Somehow the cold, gray ash reminded her of unfulfilled dreams and shipwrecked friendships. Would she ever find happiness?

# 21

# WORDS FITLY SPOKEN

*Heaviness in the heart of man maketh it stoop:*
*but a good word maketh it glad. - Proverbs 12:25*

The small, rustic church, founded by early settlers to Big Fork, resounded with sounds of laughter and friendly chatter as the women gathered for one last cup of coffee before the weekly meeting was to begin. "Ladies, ladies! May I please have your attention? It's time to be seated so our guest speakers can be introduced." Georgia, the pastor's wife, smiled at the women as they broke off from their small huddles and filed obediently into the sanctuary.

After several rousing choruses and an opening prayer, Georgia introduced the guest speakers. "Today we have the double honor of hearing the testimonies of both of these ladies who have just recently moved to our area. Rose is from Arizona, and Julie is from Oregon. Rose is also an evangelist and writer."

If Rose was aware of Julie's steady gaze upon her, she gave no notice of it. Her face, radiant and angelic, assured Julie that the women would instantly love her. Julie tried to imitate the same serene and pious expression which always seemed to make Rose popular, but Julie's face faithfully registered, and betrayed, her every thought and emotion.

Rose stood to her feet and glided to the microphone. There was an air of authority and meekness about her that brought a hush to the crowded room. Suddenly Julie saw Barbara Weston in Rose's every move. Her mannerisms, tone of voice, opening prayer; why, it was as if Barbara Weston had completely taken over the person Julie knew as Rose Miller!

Julie had seen this happen before when they had held the revival meetings Nolene had set up for them. It just hadn't really penetrated Julie's consciousness just how very much alike they were. Who was the real Barbara Weston? And who was the real Rose?

Rose's smooth voice rose and fell melodiously as she expertly wove her testimony of loneliness and suffering into a fabric of intrigue. Julie watched as one by one the women pulled tissues from their purses and pockets and wiped at their eyes.

Rose finally concluded her talk and signaled the woman in charge of the sound system with a nod of her head. Julie watched, fascinated, as the entire group was held spellbound by the anointed music.

Then it was Julie's turn to share. She felt clumsy, and awkward. How could she possibly add anything to Rose's captivating message? Placing her open Bible on the worn pulpit, she prayed for guidance. Julie knew if the Holy Spirit didn't give her the words and anointing, then she may as well skip the meeting and go fishing.

She looked up and smiled at the eager faces before her, then began a simple testimony of the grace and love of Jesus Christ. She began to feel a flow of life surging from somewhere deep within the recesses of her heart. Love and humor bubbled to the surface and overflowed into rivers of joy. Julie watched the faces before her melt into alternating expressions of laughter and thoughtfulness. One lady in particular stood out among the small sea of faces. She sat off to one side of the room and nodded thoughtfully as Julie spoke. Her dark hazel eyes sparkled with a mixture of joy and understanding. Julie felt encouraged by this young woman's receptivity.

Then the meeting was over and the small congregation gathered around Rose and Julie. "I enjoyed your testimony so much!" Julie turned and found herself looking into the face of the woman whose attentiveness had caught her attention. "You need to share more often!" she said enthusiastically.

Julie caught a glimpse of Rose out of the corner of her eye as the woman continued talking, introducing herself as Jean Jenkins. Julie nodded her thanks and tried to move away. She stiffened as small prickles of fear tingled up and down her spine. "Where are you going to be speaking next?" Jean asked, seemingly unaware of Julie's growing uneasiness.

"Oh, I don't know for sure," Julie stammered, forcing herself to give full attention to Jean. "It just depends on where the Lord opens something up." She tried to ignore the nagging thought which persistently tugged on the corners of her mind. *You're in trouble with Rose. You know Rose is going to be jealous.* The tormenting, nameless anxiety formulated into a steady barrage of accusations. *You know Rose doesn't want people to think you have a ministry. Rose wants people to believe you're just here to help her. You know Rose deserves, desires, needs to be exalted first and foremost.*

Much to Julie's dismay, the persevering Jean good-naturedly linked her arm through Julie's and drew her to one side. "I, uh," Julie said, obviously flustered, "thanks for your words of encouragement, but . . ." Julie tried to politely work her way back into throng now milling around Rose. Perhaps she could dodge Jean before Rose glared at her in disapproval. It was all to no avail, however. Jean stuck closer than a shadow, her light brown hair bouncing with every step she took. "Julie, I want to invite you, and Rose, to have lunch with me next week."

"I'll ask Rose if it's okay . . ." Julie made her way through the happy women to Rose's side. "Excuse me, Rose, I want you to meet Jean Jenkins." Rose's eyes studied the younger woman's face for a moment. Julie intently scrutinized Rose's expression. Rose's guarded eyes suddenly overflowed with compassion and warmth. She smiled broadly, put her large arm around Jean and said, "Of course, we'd love to have lunch with you."

Julie felt a pang of guilt. How could she ever think such thoughts about her wonderful minister friend? Rose was one of the best Christians she had ever met. If Rose had told her once, she had told her a thousand times: "I don't care if people know who I am or not. I just want God to receive all the glory. I am merely an ambassador for Christ."

But late that night, long after the spacious skies of Montana exchanged pastel shades of winter's sunset for the velvet curtain of night, Julie lay alone and sleepless. Strange images floated across the screen of her mind like fleeting shadows from giant clouds ripple across the distant landscape.

Throwing off the warm quilt under which she lay, Julie slipped from her bed and walked quietly to the window. Pulling aside the ruffled curtain, she peered into the vastness of the star-studded sky. "Lord, please help me. I know you walk among all those stars and call each of them by name. Please, Lord, give me strength to fulfill my promise to Rose. I want to be faithful, yet...it's so hard sometimes."

Julie stood in silence for long moments, gazing into the heavens, unaware that the ache in her heart was the same as that of an eagle held against its will.

# 22

# CHOICES

*From the end of the earth will I cry unto thee, when my heart
is overwhelmed: lead me to the rock that is higher than I. - Psalm 61:2*

It was early morning in the Jenkins' home. Jean's husband, Jack, glared over the top of his morning newspaper at his wife. Jean methodically spooned pancake batter onto a sizzling skillet. "So slow. Late again." Fully absorbed in this early morning chore and partially deafened by the humming fan above the stove, Jean failed to hear his audible complaints.

"Here are a couple more pancakes." Jean deftly slid the steaming hot breakfast onto his plate. "Can I get you more coffee?"

Jack's face hardened as a sneer appeared on his slightly parted lips. "You know I have to be leaving for work. You never get up early enough to make a decent meal for me. And," he continued, ignoring the expression of hurt registered in Jean's large eyes, "I'm sick and tired of the junk you put in my lunch!" Jack's pale blue eyes became veiled and blank. The thinning blonde hair appeared to cling to the top of his head much like seaweed, left by a retreating wave, clings to driftwood.

Jean spun around and walked to the kitchen sink. She turned on the hot water, poured liquid dish soap in the pan and began washing the dishes. She could hear Jack's heavy boots stomp

126

toward the front door. "Have my dinner ready when I get home!" Jack's voice reflected sarcasm and contempt.

Jean winced as the front door slammed and the windows rattled in response. "Lord Jesus, how I need You. Give me wisdom. Help Jack today and let him see Your love." Jean dried her hands, poured a cup of coffee and walked to the round oak table. Sinking into a chair, she began audibly reviewing her situation. "I know you tried to kill me, Jack." Jean's tone was level. She took a sip of coffee, closed her eyes and continued, "That afternoon when we went snowmobiling, I know you tried to run me off the mountain with your snowmobile." Jean cupped her fingers around the mug of hot coffee and thoughtfully said, "You will not allow me to share Christ with your unsaved family." She looked out the window. Snowflakes drifted lazily from the heavy gray clouds and clung to the bare tree branches, transforming them into lacy fingers of white. "And," Jean added somberly, "Jack, let's face it: you don't really respect, appreciate, or…or…love me."

Jean stood to her feet and returned to the kitchen sink. She leaned toward the small window and scanned the horizon. The jagged outline of the Rocky Mountains was quickly fading from view as the falling snow intensified. "Well, Lord, you know all about it. I'm trusting in You to deliver me from an angry man and help me to make the right choices."

The shrill ring of the telephone permeated the chilly air. Jean's slippers made a soft scuffling sound as she hurried across the pale blue linoleum. "Good morning!" Jean's voice was cheerful, giving no hint of the tumultuous thoughts churning within her heart.

A kind male voice responded on the other end of the line. "Good morning, Jean. This is Pastor John. Georgia and I would like to see you today, if that would be possible. The Lord has put you on our hearts, and we want to encourage you and pray with you."

Jean's face softened with relief. "Oh Pastor, that would be wonderful! God is so good! I really need to talk to you. I'll get dressed and just walk on over if that's okay with you. Jack's using my truck because his is in the garage being worked on."

The genuine warmth and love in Pastor John's voice gave Jean a sense of security and hope. She quickly showered and bundled up in a bright, red sweater, and gray wool slacks. Pulling on her snow boots, she chuckled out loud. "Thank You Lord, for having Pastor John call. Georgia is sure blessed to have a husband like him. He knows how to love his wife!"

The short walk to the parsonage was invigorating to Jean. The air was fresh and still. Insistent snowflakes fluttered and swirled about her, clinging to her down jacket and plaid scarf.

As Jean turned up the walkway to the parsonage, the front door flew open and both Pastor John and Georgia stepped out onto the small porch to welcome Jean. Loving arms enveloped her, reassuring her that she was understood, accepted, loved. "Come on in and sit here by the fire," bubbled Georgia enthusiastically. "John and I were just about to have an omelet and blueberry muffins. Would you care to join us? I made plenty, hoping you'd say 'yes'." Georgia was short and pleasingly plump. She had short curly, blonde hair which had a way of slightly bouncing when she spoke. Her round face beamed with joy.

Jean had to laugh. Georgia always made people feel like part of the family. "Of course, I'd love to eat with you two."

The meal was an enjoyable time of good fellowship and food. Pastor John laid his big hand over his wife's and complimented her cooking. Jean watched them with longing. If only Jack would treat her half as good, she would follow him anywhere.

"Well, let's retreat to the fire and have a good visit," Pastor John said as he stood and pushed back his chair. He carried his dishes to the kitchen sink, and then turned toward the living room. Jean had always found it interesting that, for a pastor, John had such a muscular build. Besides spending long hours in his study, he always managed to find time to hike, hunt, and chop wood, much of which he shared with others. The men of the church admired and respected him and accepted him as one of them.

"Jean," Pastor John began. His kind face reflected the love of Christ, but there was something somber in his normally twinkling, brown eyes. "I am going to get right to the point," he said softly. "Georgia and I are not unaware of the situation in your home." He cleared his throat and continued, "Jack is someone both of us have known for a long time. As you know, we knew him before he married you."

Jean nodded in agreement. Georgia reached over and patted her reassuringly on the knee. "You need to know," Pastor John's voice contained a note of urgency, "that we are concerned for you, Jean."

Jean sat forward in her chair and opened her mouth to speak, but he held up a hand to silence her. "You need to be careful, Jean. Jack is an angry man and the Bible warns about keeping company with angry or violent people."

Jean stared down at her hands, which were folded in her lap. "So," she said slowly, groping for the right words, "you know."

"Yes, I'm afraid we do," Georgia answered sweetly.

"I mean, how did you know . . .?" Her voice trailed off.

"Jack has quite a reputation, Jean," Pastor John said. He leaned forward and peered into her downcast face. "Now, I know he comes to church and puts on a big show, but he doesn't fool us. We know what's going on in his mind, and we know what he's capable of."

Suddenly a cold chill sent shivers down Jean's spine. It was one thing to have an idea that your husband would like to do away with you, but it was another thing to be faced with the certainty of it. Having someone else voice what you already knew made it somehow more real, more terrifying. Jean sucked in her breath.

"What should I do? I know the Bible says we are to honor our marriage vows." She looked up helplessly, then added, "You're right. He's already tried some things, I mean, to make it look like an accident."

Georgia sat up straight and looked at her husband. The expression on her face shouted, "See, I told you so!"

"Jean," Pastor John's voice was understanding, "Jesus never asked His women to put their lives in danger where their husbands were concerned. We know you've lived the Christian life before Jack. We know you've fasted and prayed and interceded for his soul. But we also know," he said with conviction borne from hours spent in study and prayer, "that God is not asking you to be a dead sacrifice for the sake of Jack. That's not the way God works."

Jean blinked back tears. "Then," she rasped, "what am I going to do?"

For the remainder of the day, Pastor John and Georgia prayed with Jean. They lovingly counseled her and affirmed they were there for her should she ever need help. The hours flew, and much to Jean's dismay, the subdued light of the short winter day had given way to darker tones of evening before she stood to leave. Her face reflected a mixture of hope, love, sorrow, and determination. "Thank you, Pastor and Georgia. I know God brought us together today. I appreciate your understanding and sound counsel. I realize the choice is mine, and I've already made that choice. In fact, I made it a long time ago, and I guess Jack always knew that. I will serve the Lord Jesus no matter what happens."

After saying a final prayer together, Jean walked the short distance toward her home. Streetlights flickered and sparked to life as the fading light of day vanished in the West. Snatches of the day's conversation pulsated through her mind, punctuated only by deliberate pleas to God for help. The frigid night air was hushed and still except for the rhythmic scrunch, scrunch of Jean's boots as she made her way through the white wonderland.

"Where on earth have you been? Where's my dinner?" Jack's voice boomed across the long expanse of sparkling snow which carpeted their front lawn and ricocheted off the stately trees standing proud and silent like soldiers on guard. His large frame filled the open doorway, silhouetted by the bright light behind him. His tousled hair was bunched crazily on top of his head. Jean couldn't make out his dark features, but she could picture his eyes, cunning and cruel, and the wide mouth twisted in a wicked smirk. Somewhere in the back of her mind she thought he resembled a huge gorilla, poised to attack. Her strained nerves and pent-up emotions suddenly wanted to cave in with hysterical laughter. Instead, she heard her voice steadily reply, "Jack, I've been at Pastor's place. Why don't we go to the café tonight and have dinner together?" Jean paused, hoping against hope her irate husband would soften in agreement.

"Are you kidding?" he roared. Steam from his breath hung in the frozen air like little puffs from a dragon. "I don't want to spend my hard-earned money eating out! Get in here and cook dinner!" He turned away from the doorway, walked with a jerk into the living room and flipped on the television. Jean's heart sank as she took off her boots and coat. The macabre sounds of a bloody war movie boomed through the house.

"Lord," Jean whispered, "forgive me for not listening to You five years ago when I said 'yes' to this man. But You know, Jesus, I met him in church. He said he was born again. I made a bad choice. Now I must make another choice. What should it be?"

But even as Jean softly spoke, she already knew the answer in her heart.

# 23

# GONE!

*. . . for the Lord hath heard the*
*voice of my weeping. - Psalm 6:8*

"Wow! This is our day! Look at all the mail!" Julie exuberantly waltzed across the small living room to Rose who quietly lay in her recliner.  She looked up expectantly.

"Anything from the kids?" Her voice was filled with longing.

Julie handed the soft pink envelope to Rose. "And guess who else?" Before Rose could reply, Julie continued. "I got a letter from Mom and there's even one from Patsy!"

Rose's eyes widened slightly. "Patsy!  She hasn't written since we were in Phoenix months ago. Let me see!" Julie obligingly gave the welcome letter to Rose. Secretly, she wanted to open it herself, but she was relieved to see Rose suddenly perk up. Lately Rose had become silent and withdrawn. She spent long hours at Melody's, and even though Julie was always invited, she felt the pressure to accomplish something, which usually meant working long hours in her art studio. Julie still taught an occasional class in the hobby shop along with monthly workshops. The financial situation had not improved, but neither had the women gone hungry.

Lately a persistent, unpleasant, and unwelcome thought intruded into Julie's mind and heart. It began by subtly pushing

132

against the deep recesses of her soul, almost undetectably at first, like the distant thunder when it rolled beyond the towering mountains just before it suddenly swept over the peaceful valley. She fought against it, vainly trying to keep the ugly truth from invading her ordered thought patterns. But it would descend unexpectedly, wrapping its oppressive darkness around her with cords of fear. *What if,* it hissed into her heart, *what if Rose doesn't want you in her ministry anymore? What if she decides to return to the desert and live with her kids? What if . . .?*

Julie took a deep breath and began to read the small note from Catherine. *Dear Julie, I hope this finds you. I never really know for sure where you are these days. It's been raining here in Portland. I suppose it is cold and snowing over there. When are you going to come for a visit? Are you going to get a regular job? You really should think about doing something that makes money. Don't have any more news. Love, Mom. PS Here's $5. Go out for tea someday and pretend I'm there with you.*

Julie fingered the crumpled bill and looked at Rose who was totally absorbed in Donna's letter. Julie noted there were tears in her eyes. A sharp stab of fear tore at her heart as Julie asked herself, *How long can Rose bear to be without her grown children?* Julie grimaced slightly as she thought about the recent confrontations she and Rose had had regarding Rose's children.

"Julie," Rose had stated firmly, you never had kids so you just don't understand." Julie had shot back, "That doesn't make any difference, Rose! Jesus said if you want to follow Him, then you have to be willing to part with family members. Besides, her voice raised, your kids aren't kids anymore! They are adults who are making their own choices, who have their own lives to live!"

Julie recalled how livid Rose was. She had stomped out of the house, got in her car and roared down the dirt driveway, out onto the gravel road, and off to Melody's house. Julie, for once, was glad she was gone. She needed time with the Lord, time to regain her perspective.

Rose stirred in her recliner and Julie glanced over at her. She was nodding and smiling. She gently folded the letter and, ignoring Julie's questioning gaze, tore open the envelope from Patsy. Softly she read aloud, "Dear Rose and Julie, Daniel and I miss you both so much and hope your ministry is going well." Julie's lips pressed together in an expression of disgust. *What ministry?* She thought. *If only you knew, Patsy, that Rose spends most of her time slouched in her chair or down at Melody's. I can't get her to write a newsletter, book meetings, or finish her book.*

Rose looked sharply at Julie as if somehow reading her mind, then continued with Patsy's letter. "When are you going to come back to Dayport? I really need you. I'm trying to put together a home meeting, but I'm working more at the café and am tired most of the time. I haven't even had time to paint and miss the art classes. Perhaps we could paint at my place if you can come to Dayport, or are you planning to spend the winter in Arizona with Rose's children?" Rose hesitated briefly before continuing. "I saw Gary the other day down on the beach. He had the brunette woman with him and they were holding hands. I'm enclosing $30 to help you in ministry. Please call me collect so we can talk! Love always, Patsy."

"Oh, I miss Patsy so much," Julie fought against homesickness. "But, Lord willing, perhaps we will be able to go to Oregon for meetings next summer."

Rose leaned back in the chair, closed her eyes and sighed deeply. "What's the matter, Rose? Are you feeling sick?" Julie determined to extract every thought Rose presently had. Rose sighed again. An unsolicited spark of anger reflected in Julie's voice. "Rose, what . . ."

"Here!" Rose flung Donna's letter at Julie. "Read this!" Julie unfolded the pastel paper and eagerly scanned the contents.

"Dear Mama," it began, "please, please, please come home. We all need you! Ralph and I are getting married in two weeks and you have to be here. I miss you. Come back to where you are loved. Don't mention I said anything to you, but Duane is in trouble and needs to talk to you. Anyway, Ralph and I are going to buy a house and he agreed to fix up a room just for you. Please call me soon. Love you until the end of time, Donna."

Julie's heart pounded out of control and her head spun crazily. Even though she knew what the outcome would be, she had to try. "Rose, we can't leave now for Arizona! We just plain don't have the money! Besides, there isn't one open door for ministry down there..."

"Stop it, Julie!" Rose cut in. "You just don't understand because you don't have children. You don't even like children!" Her words were hard and cold, resembling driving rain that slashes and stings at an unprotected face. "I'm sorry I ever let you read the letter."

*Here we go again,* Julie thought as Rose snatched the letter from Julie's trembling fingers. She pushed her large frame out of the recliner and walked to where her jacket lay. "I'll be at Melody's."

The next few days were filled with a whirlwind of activity as Rose prepared for the long trip south. The incident surrounding Donna's letter was never mentioned again, and Rose's attitude toward Julie measurably improved. Plans were made for Julie to finish her art commitments, travel in the motor home to Dayport for the Christmas holidays, and then journey south to meet Rose in Phoenix. In the meantime, a list of several churches had been made which Julie was to contact for possible meetings in Arizona.

Julie braced herself for the trauma of being alone. The one thing she feared most was about to befall her, and she knew her relationship with Christ was all that would sustain her in the days and weeks to come.

"Well, my friend," Rose rested her hands on Julie's sagging shoulders. "The time has come. You'll be okay here. You have the Lord, Melody, and the Davis family. And," she suddenly brightened as if struck with a brilliant idea, "Get a hold of that Jean woman in town. She likes you a lot." Rose turned and picked up an overstuffed suitcase, then turned back to look at Julie. "Julie," her eyes radiated an unusual and compelling light, "I really appreciate you. Thanks for fixing up my car."

Julie's face registered a blend of relief and bewilderment. As if to establish lasting assurance, Rose added benignly, "I need you. I always will."

Then she was gone, leaving Julie alone in the pale shadows of dawn.

# 24

# BURDEN BEARER

*Come unto me, all ye that labor and are heavy laden,*
*and I will give you rest. - Matthew 11:28*

Somewhere in that dimension between deep sleep and wakefulness it came. It wasn't an illusion, but neither was it a dream. The single stream of light flowed from an unseen heavenly origin. Its brilliant shaft culminated around a single figure. As Julie's attention focused on the image, her spiritual ear distinctly heard these words: "Take care of my servant, Jean." Then the figure became recognizable . . . the short brown hair, the flawless complexion and intelligent eyes filled with both determination and a plea for help. Suddenly the vision was gone and Julie found herself wide awake.

"I've got to get going, got to call Jean." She threw back the quilt and swung out of bed. Since Rose's departure it had been hard for Julie to rouse herself. She felt like a punctured balloon and forced herself to drag through each day's monotonous routine in silent resignation. She felt suspended in a void without purpose or meaning. The only time her spirits lifted was when she was able to share Christ with one of her art students.

She flipped through the address book. "Jean Jenkins, here it is," she muttered. She punched in Jean's number and waited. One, two, three, four rings. *Where could she go this early in the morning?* Julie thought. Suddenly the ringing stopped and Jean's friendly voice was on the other end of the line with a cheerful, "Good morning."

"Hello, Jean?" Julie's voice sounded husky, clueing Jean in on the lateness of Julie's departure from her bed. "How are you doing?" She squinted at the kitchen clock. It was 8:30 a.m.

Jean's voice, as usual, was friendly and steady. "I've had better days, to tell you the truth, but the Lord will see me through. You sound anxious about something. What is it?"

Julie hesitated for a moment, and then gave a brief summary of her vision. She could hear Jean suck in her breath. Finally, she gave a short laugh but her tone was serious. "Julie, I . . . I'm so glad the Lord did this. I'm in trouble, that's for sure. Jack told me to 'take a hike' last night. His reservoir of anger scares me. I don't know how long he's going to be able to control it before he finally explodes."

"Jean," Julie sounded suddenly alert. "Listen to me. I'm all alone here for at least another two weeks. Then I have to make sure this place is winterized, and I'm going to Oregon for the holidays and then down to Arizona to help Rose with her ministry. If you need to come here, day or night, you are more than welcome!" Julie sensed Jean's relief.

"What happened to Rose?" Jean asked, changing the subject. "I didn't know she was gone."

Julie paused, groping for the facts. *Just stick to the facts, Julie,* she told herself, *and don't go blabbing off your big mouth about all your feelings.* "Rose had to tend to some family business, and I couldn't go because I have to finish my art obligations, and then we'll minister later in Arizona." Julie's words tumbled from her mouth resembling one long string of beads.

"Oh, I see," Jean answered thoughtfully. "Well, thanks for calling, Julie. I have to go now. But I'll be in touch."

The conversation ended. Julie dressed, nibbled on an apple and then prepared to put the finishing touches on the last oil painting she had to complete. She was still painting when the full moon rose high in the inky Montana sky. Painting was the one activity Julie could lose herself in. Gusts of wind hammered the old house, muffling the sound of a car pulling into the gravel driveway. Julie visibly jumped at the sound of loud thumping and knocking pounded on the front door. "Who could that be this late hour?" She forced her voice to sound bold in a vain attempt to overcome the prickles of fear crawling up her spine. Being all alone, especially at night, had never been Julie's idea of how one should live.

A familiar voice rang out, "Julie! It's me! Jean!" Julie sighed with relief and flung open the weather-beaten door. A giant gust of wind puffed into the room, ruffling the curtains.

"Jean, wha-a-a— "Julie stammered. Jean's usually calm eyes were wide with anguish and fear.

"Julie," she blurted out, "he flipped! I mean, Jack came unglued. He's literally possessed!" She dropped into a chair and covered her face with her hands.

Julie quickly shut and locked the door and went to Jean's side. She began to pray, "O, Jesus, comfort Jean at this time and give her strength. Comfort her, Lord Jesus. Thank you, Lord."

"Thanks," Jean smiled gratefully. "I'm sorry to barge in on you like this. I mean, so late and everything. But thank God, He chose you to be here when I needed help."

Julie grinned, "Yeah, He's got it all figured out, doesn't He? Hey! How about a hot cup of tea and a tuna sandwich?"

Jean nodded eagerly. "Great! I'd like that. I've been so upset I haven't eaten much all day. While you're in the kitchen fixing things up, I think I'll unload a few personal things from my car. Is that okay with you?"

"Well, of course! I told you before, I'm here for you. Make yourself at home!"

Julie busied herself in the kitchen while Jean went to retrieve the few items she had managed to take with her. She had gathered the small bundle of clothes and her Bible when suddenly headlights flashed into Julie's driveway. Jean gasped, nearly dropping her belongings. Someone must have been parked at the end of the lane, waiting, watching. Jean's heart began to hammer in her head. "Jack!" she gasped. "He must've followed me."

Just then Julie stepped out onto the porch. "Hey Jean, hurry, get in here!" She called. Jean lost no time in responding. Tearing her eyes from the pair of bright lights, she dashed across the grass and bounded up the steps. Both women hurried through the door and quickly bolted it shut. Julie turned the indoor lights off so they could peek out the window at the unwelcome intruder. The lights flashed off and on as if giving some sort of signal. Suddenly the vehicle backed up onto the road, lurched to a stop, pulled forward and tore down the road until it was out of sight.

"Whew!" Jean said, dropping onto the couch. Julie pulled the curtains closer together and turned on a dim light.

"Wait until I bring in our snack," Julie said in a shaky voice, "and then you can tell me all about Jack." She walked into the kitchen. Her legs felt as if they were made of rubber and her mind bounced like a ping pong ball gone wild. Suddenly Rose flashed on the screen of her mind. She felt dizzy and braced herself against the counter, trying to clear her thoughts. *Julie,* she admitted to herself, *you're not afraid of Jack. You're afraid of Rose.* A mental image of herself in a small boat being helplessly carried downstream on a rampaging river flanked by towering cliffs invaded her mind. Without a doubt, the one canyon wall was Rose, and the other, Jean. She shook herself and spoke aloud for her own benefit, "What a strange way to think."

She finished making the sandwiches, poured two cups of steaming hot tea from the only teapot Rose had let her keep, and started for the living room. *God definitely spoke to me about Jean.*

Julie mentally calculated. *And I must do what the Lord has told me to do regardless of the outcome with Rose. And,* she reasoned, *if Rose is truly a Christian, then she will be more than willing to accept Jean's presence, at least temporarily.*

"There," Julie stated cheerfully as she placed the tray of small sandwiches on the beaten second-hand coffee table. "And here's some herb tea that's supposed to be relaxing!"

"Thanks. This looks great." Jean reached for a sandwich. "I didn't realize just how hungry I was." She took a bite, closed her eyes as if it was the most wonderful gourmet food she'd ever tasted. "Today was awful. I never had time to stop and eat." Jean took a sip of tea and continued, "Jack, well, actually the devil, manifested tonight. Satan is bizarre, gross!" she said breathlessly. "Pastor John and Georgia are gone for a couple of days. I had no place to go and I can't tell you how much I appreciate being able to come here, believe me!"

Julie related much of what had taken place between her and Gary before their divorce. Jean listened attentively and then shared her experiences with Jack. It was two o'clock in the morning before the two friends bid one another "good night."

But long after Jean had settled in Rose's vacant room, Julie lay thinking of the strange twists and turns in her life. All she had wanted was to serve God, to be loved, and to have some measure of security. *So far,* she solemnly concluded, *all I've done is fail at all three. Of course,* she told herself, *you need to trust God's love and forget worldly security. God will provide somehow. And His love far outweighs that of any fleshly husband, even though sometimes I really wish I had one.* She turned restlessly under the heavy layer of blankets. Thoughts continued to present themselves, pushing sleep far from her. *Then there's the matter of service to God. It's so hard to get into churches to minister. I've worked in the church, for the church and with the church. But the church has not once encouraged or supported my calling to minister for the Lord. It's like a club. If you belong to the club, then you can operate within its rules and regulations. But if you, under the inspiration and direction of God, are called to work outside of the club, then you're shut out. I don't get it.* Julie flipped to her back and lay staring into the dark. *What is real ministry, Lord?* Without waiting for an answer, Julie answered the question herself. *Lift up the fallen, provide shelter for the homeless, provide food, water, and clothes for those in need, pray for the sick, preach the gospel, cast out demons, weep with those that weep, rejoice with those who rejoice, and do unto others as you would have them do unto you.*

"Lord," Julie whispered into darkness, "I want to do these things, but how?" The answer came before Julie stopped speaking. *Be faithful with that which is right before you. Be faithful with the small things, and you will be entrusted with more.*

Julie smiled. Yes, she was right where the Lord wanted her. For some reason known only to God, Jean was what He was asking her to be faithful with. Assured of God's presence and protection, Julie finally fell into a deep sleep.

# 25

# PAVING THE WAY

*Be kindly affectioned one to another with brotherly love;*
*in honour preferring one another. - Romans 12:10*

Julie's mind spun crazily. How quickly things had changed! It had been six weeks since that blustery, dark night when Jean fled from Jack to the old Montana house. Ever since Jean's decision to accompany Julie to Oregon and ultimately through California, their lives had been a whirlwind of activity.

Melody's brother had congenially agreed to winterize the house. Julie knew once they left Montana, it would be months before they would be able to return. Nevertheless, rent was expected to be paid on time. Julie trusted that somehow the Lord would bring the necessary money in.

Julie had bid Nolene and Hank "good bye" with the promise of writing to let them know how the ministry was doing. Jean, at the same time, hugged Pastor John and Georgia farewell. It was an emotional time for her, but she eagerly looked forward to the walk of faith before her. Jack had driven past Julie's house a few times and made a few phone calls to Jean. His conversations carried veiled threats, but Jean simply referred him to her Christian attorney.

Julie had wanted to spend Christmas with Catherine, but after a short afternoon visit in Portland with her mother, Catherine and her husband flew to Hawaii to be with friends. Jean knew Julie was both hurt and disappointed, but Julie assured her perhaps it was best this way. Catherine still did not accept Rose or Julie's decision to follow Christ in ministry.

Their short time in Dayport was hectic. Jean was introduced to Patsy and Daniel, who enthusiastically greeted her. It was a time of joyful reunion for Julie, who laughed and cried at the same time as she hugged them. It was obvious to Jean that Julie loved them both very much.

It was Ruth who offered Julie and Jean a place to stay. She loved to cook and bake and spent most of her time "sputtering and puttering," as Julie called it, in her warm kitchen. She giggled and laughed and was genuinely happy to see Julie. It had been a long time.

Julie's heart longed for time alone on the beach, but Jean stuck to her like glue. *I don't think Rose is going to appreciate a third party, especially one whom she didn't choose,* Julie thought glumly as she and Jean jumped out of the RV and onto the sandy parking lot. *But I can't help this situation at all! And, I didn't want to travel all alone anyway! It's just not safe these days.*

The time in Dayport was bitter-sweet for Julie. "Are you okay?" Jean's hazel eyes searched Julie's face. "You look sort of depressed."

"I'm fine, Jean. Don't worry. It's just kind of hard coming back here. I mean, it reminds me of Gary and the hard time the church gave me. You know, all those things I told you about on our trip out here."

"I understand," Jean said sympathetically.

Julie lifted her face into the stout, cold wind. She sniffed at the salty smell, and laughed. "I love it here," she exclaimed. "I forgot how wonderful it is on this wild, woolly beach!"

"I can see how hard it was for you to leave this beautiful place," Jean commented. "I think this is a wonderful place to come and pray."

"Yeah," Julie said wistfully. "It can't be beat. I'll have to take you up to see the *Sea Queen* before we leave for Arizona."

The girls walked along the sandy shore for a couple of hours, talking, praying, sharing hopes and dreams. A sudden squall caught them off guard and they raced for the motor home.

"Whew!" Julie said as she shed her wet jacket. She glanced at her watch. "We better get back to Ruth's. She's expecting us for dinner."

The women busied themselves at Ruth's house calling several pastors and churches in Arizona. It was hard, time-consuming work. Julie spent hours with follow-up calls, but finally booked Rose into a church in Flagstaff and two revivals near Prescott. The atmosphere in Ruth's home was tense during those times when Julie was making calls trying to work up ministry. It was obvious Ruth had not budged one iota in her opinion of Rose.

There was so much Julie wanted to show Jean, and she wished she could spend more time with Patsy and Daniel. Everyone, it seemed, was buried in Christmas preparations. *People go on with their lives,* Julie thought sadly. *Even though they weep and cry when you leave them, they soon forget and go on.*

Two days after Christmas, the weather report confirmed that the way through the mountains between southern Oregon and northern California was clear. The girls hurriedly straightened the small motor home, had the oil changed, and prepared to leave. Ruth waved a tearful farewell, and they were off.

"Here we go, Jean!" Julie said as she pulled away from the curb. "I hope you enjoyed your visit to Dayport."

Jean nodded and smiled. "I had a wonderful time and a wonderful Christmas, even though it was just the two of us." Ruth

145

had gone out to have dinner with relatives, leaving Julie and Jean alone.

"I'm so glad we were together," Julie added thoughtfully. "I would've been pretty depressed all by myself." Her mind replayed the phone conversation she had had with Rose on Christmas day. Julie knew she would probably be at Donna's, and her hunch paid off. Rose sounded different somehow. Maybe it was just because there were so many people coming and going from Donna's house. Julie tried to recall Rose's exact words. *You are coming down here with Jean?* There had been a long pause. Julie had clearly explained Jean's circumstances. Julie was sure Rose had said, *You don't need to come down to Arizona. I can handle the meetings by myself.* Julie had been thunderstruck. The background din muffled Rose's soft voice. Julie raised her voice so Rose could hear her. "Rose, I'll call you from California. Okay?"

"All right then," Rose had stated flatly. "I have to go." Click. The phone went dead.

The trip through Oregon and into California was pleasant and uneventful. Jean chatted happily about how she had longed to be free to serve the Lord and how she was willing to do anything she could to help Rose and Julie.

"Well, we're getting closer," Julie said wearily as she pulled into a rest area close to Yreka. "I better give Rose a call."

Jean leaned against the phone booth and watched Julie dial Donna's number. "You are where?" Rose inquired on the other end of the line. Julie's grip tightened on the receiver as she repeated, "Jean and I are just outside Yreka, California. We should be in Arizona in a couple of days if all goes well. It's hard to push the motor home too fast. We're loaded and . . ."

"Julie," Rose interrupted, "Please tell me again the dates of the meetings you set up and where they are. I'm ready to write them down."

146

Julie gave the dates and places for the three churches in Arizona. She absentmindedly glanced up at Jean. A knowing look crossed her kind face. Julie turned and gave Rose the requested information. "Got it?" she asked. Julie knew Rose had no idea of the hours she and Jean had spent contacting dozens of pastors trying to secure meetings. Then there was the additional work of photocopying Rose's letters of recommendation which had to be mailed along with a follow up letter.

"Thanks. Now I've got to get busy and prepare my messages. Hey, Julie! I need some money for expenses. Think you can send me $150 right away?"

Julie sucked in her breath. It had taken nearly every dollar she had left to pay rent in advance to Melody, purchase insurance, new tires and gasoline for the motor home, pay for postage, food, and the other necessities of life. "Just a minute, Rose," Julie clamped her hand over the mouthpiece and motioned to Jean. "Ps-s-s-s-t, Jean. Rose needs money to get to the meetings we set up. What do you think . . .?"

"That's okay. I've got my savings yet. We'll just take it out of that." Jean smiled reassuringly at Julie.

"Okay, Rose. Jean will write out a check for you. She's been such a terrific help. I know the Lord sent her to us, not only so we could help her get through a bad situation, but she is also helping us. And," she added breathlessly, "Pray for supporters."

"Julie," Rose's voice sounded strained, "Are you sure you should come down to Arizona? I mean, I can drive to the meetings myself, and Debbie and Duane can go with me. Anyway, to be honest with you, I'm not sure Jean is ready for ministry yet. She's gone through so much and..."

"Wait a minute, Rose!" Julie could feel her face grow hot. "We're already on our way, for one thing. Secondly, we're coming to help you with your meetings and the book table. Plus, I have some of my Christian paintings with me that I desperately need to sell. And," she swallowed hard, then continued, "You approved of Jean coming when we called you from Dayport. I can't just sit here for the rest of the winter."

"Well," Rose's voice had a strange ring to it, "It costs a lot of money to drive that motor home down here, and there's no place to park it. But if you do come, please call me when you get near Flagstaff. I've got to go. Donna and Ralph are taking me out to eat. Pray for me! Bye."

Julie's head spun and she felt sick to her stomach. "You look awful!" Jean exclaimed. "What's the matter? Is everything all right?"

"It's Rose. She, uh, she wonders if it's in our best interest to continue this trip." Tears formed in Julie's tired eyes. "I haven't seen her for over two months! We're supposed to be a team..." The unbidden tears flowed down her flushed cheeks.

"It's okay. God is in control. I know we're supposed to go to Arizona and help with those meetings. Don't worry so much! I have money yet and God will provide. You'll see! Come on, let's go pray for a while." She led the way toward the I motor home.

Morning came softly with warm shades of pastel. Julie wakened to the sound of birds chirping to one another in the nearby pine trees. Her heart fluttered with excitement. Finally, she was close to seeing Rose again. She and Jean had developed a special friendship, yet Julie was convinced with every fiber of her being it was God's will that she was a team with Rose.

Soon the eager travelers drove through the scenic countryside that seemed to change by the hour. Their animated conversation reviewed events surrounding Jack, visits with Catherine in Portland and with Patsy, Daniel, and Ruth while in Oregon. They talked about the Bible and the Lord. Julie's amazement at Jean's depth and wisdom turned to genuine respect and admiration. Somehow, she knew Jean had a special calling on her life. Rose was also a topic of conversation.

"I can hardly wait until we all meet in Flagstaff." Excitement rang in Jean's voice. "It's so exciting to know we'll be working together for the Lord."

Julie nodded silently as she maneuvered the RV around a sharp bend in the narrow road. Tension, which at first had only timidly tried to burrow its way into her mind, now seemed to gain a stranglehold. Julie tried to mentally shake herself. *What is the matter with you, Julie Danza?* Perhaps by scolding herself she would be able to push out these alien invaders who insisted on forcing unwanted anxieties upon her. *You know very well Rose often mentioned needing help, that we needed a team.* Another voice argued, *But you know very well Rose meant her kids when she spoke of a team.*

". . . and all I really want to do is be a servant and to help you and Rose in ministry." Jean's sprightly discourse broke through Julie's mental battle.

"Yes," Julie heard herself reply absently, "It's going to be wonderful when we finally get to Arizona." But deep within the hidden recesses of her own heart a tortuous voice mockingly echoed, *You're in trouble, Julie. Big trouble.*

# 26

# STING OF THE THORN

*For it was not an enemy that reproached me;
then I could have borne it…" - Psalm 55:12*

"Enjoy your meal." The smiling waitress turned and walked briskly to another booth. The stocky, well-built pastor and his petite wife turned to Julie and Jean. "We're sure looking forward to meeting Rose when she gets into Flagstaff," Pastor Manning said as he sipped his iced tea.

"Yes," chorused his wife, Martha, "We ran an ad in the local paper advertising a series of revival meetings. Our people are inviting others to come, too."

Jean spoke up with enthusiasm, "Rose does have a way of sharing new insights from scripture. But Julie is an evangelist too. You should hear her testimony!"

"Well, we'll have to set aside some time just for that." Pastor Manning grinned at Julie. "Testimonies of what the Lord Jesus is doing in our lives are a vital part of our church." His gray eyes twinkled with joy.

Julie's face colored noticeably with embarrassment. Sometimes Jean's exuberance made her uncomfortable. Rose's conduct in the presence of church leaders was always reserved and subdued, giving Julie the impression that Rose possessed superior understanding and wisdom where the clergy were concerned.

"We want to thank you again for allowing us to park the RV next to the church." Julie picked up her fork, laid the napkin in her lap and continued. "Hookups and all! It sure makes things nice for us." She poked uneasily at a hunk of lettuce with her fork and added, "Rose should be here tomorrow afternoon to meet us."

Later that night, long after Jean fell asleep, Julie lay thinking about Rose. Conflicting emotions warred against one another. With all her heart she wanted to fling open the motor home door and dash off into the night. But running away wasn't going to solve the problems she faced. How was she going to strike a balance between Rose and Jean, whom God had placed in her life? Tears trickled down her cheeks and saturated her pillow. Somehow in her spirit she knew her relationship with Rose was changing. And, what about ministry? Julie's heart quickened with stabs of fear. Without Rose, she didn't have a "ministry." Rose was the evangelist. Rose was the one with the vision and the call. True, Julie knew God had placed His hand upon her, but that must be for the far distant future. She had watched Rose conduct meetings, lead altar calls, pray for people. She was not prepared to be on her own—not yet.

Somehow sleep mercifully overcame Julie's churning ruminations and she didn't waken until nine-thirty in the morning. "Jean, Jean! Oh, there you are!" Jean sat quietly reading her Bible. Julie yawned, threw back the covers and said, "We have to get ready. Rose will be here in a few hours!"

Jean grinned at her disheveled friend. "I thought you needed to rest. We've been really pushing it lately." She closed the worn Bible, sipped her coffee and continued, "You know, I'm so thankful God put us together. I've always wanted to live by faith, and now I get to do it!"

Julie sighed. "Jean, it's not fun. Believe me, it's much easier to talk about living by faith than it is to do, and . . ." Julie jumped as loud knocks rattled the small door. "Who?" Julie squinted through a crack in the curtains by the kitchen table. "Oh no! It's Rose already! I'm not up yet!" Julie grabbed her robe and hurried to the door. Throwing it open she babbled, "Rose! It's so good to see you . . ."

"Hi, Julie. Hi Jean." Rose smiled faintly and gave a nervous chuckle as she stepped into the crowded space. Her eyes scrutinized the interior of the RV. Then she patted Julie on the shoulder and Jean on the hand. "I see you're not ready to go out yet, so I'm going on over and meet the Mannings and then perhaps we can visit later." She turned to go.

"Rose. Wait! I haven't seen you for months! Can't you wait? Have a cup of coffee? We need to talk, to discuss the meetings!" Julie felt her heartbeat quicken. Rose seemed so casual, almost cold. Or, was it just Julie's imagination? She felt suddenly awkward, ugly, stupid.

Rose hesitated briefly. "Julie, umm, come here a second." She motioned for Julie to follow her to the doorway. Once outside, Rose turned and studied Julie's bewildered countenance. "Julie, I need to speak with you alone," Rose whispered tersely. "I'll meet you at the Flagstaff Café in half an hour." She spun on her heel and walked briskly toward the church.

Julie ignored Jean's questioning gaze as she probed through the small, over-crowded closet. "Where's my green blouse?" she murmured to herself. "Ah, there you are!" Gathering up her clothes, Julie shut herself in the cramped bathroom, leaving Jean to ponder this latest turn of events alone.

Guilt, frustration, fear, and anger revolved in her mind like merry-go-round horses chasing one another. However, she resolved to maintain a calm composure and trust God for the outcome. Twenty-five minutes later she emerged looking more confident than she felt.

Jean looked up and said, "I am praying for you." She smiled knowingly.

"Thanks. I need it. I probably won't be long." She grabbed her purse and stepped out the door.

It was three blocks to the brightly painted red and white café. Julie walked briskly. Each step on the pavement became a staccato rhythm in her ears. Her lively imagination painted a picture of herself marching to Ravel's "Bolero." The imaginary music abruptly ended as Julie stepped up to the door of the cheerful café. She pushed it open with renewed determination and glanced around the crowded room.

Rose was already seated in a corner booth with a cup of coffee. Julie slid into the narrow seat opposite her friend. Rose's eyes held Julie in their fathomless depths. Compassion, sorrow, and something she couldn't identify seemed to flow from those hazel pools into the far reaches of her soul.

"How have you been?" Rose's casual demeanor totally caught Julie off guard. What a trite question after all those long weeks apart.

Julie heard herself stammer idiotically, "Uh, oh, fine."

They were interrupted by the waiter, who quickly took their order and left. Once again Rose and Julie faced each other. Julie felt queasy and strange. It was as if the small table between them somehow represented an invisible Grand Canyon.

"Julie," Rose shifted her weight uncomfortably. She stared for a moment into her coffee as if somehow the dark liquid held the words she was groping for. "The Lord has shown me some things."

Julie stiffened. It was always easy to blame the Lord when people didn't know how to make decisions for themselves. Rose continued without emotion, "I know what you and Jean have been doing. I know you've been working together to undermine my ministry and build one of your own."

The shock which spread over Julie's features caused several customers to stare in her direction. She tried to keep her voice low and calm. "Rose, that's just not true! How could you say such a thing! Jean and I have worked diligently to secure these meetings for you! All we have done or intend to do is help your ministry! We don't have…"

The waiter stood patiently to one side waiting for an opportunity to ask if Rose wanted more coffee. She smiled at him and nodded in gratitude. He filled her cup and left. Rose leveled her gaze on Julie. "Well, I happen to know it's true. The Lord showed me! Besides that," she added with a hiss, "You have a spirit of control."

Julie gasped as she watched Rose's eyes. The usual calm and harmless glow which had always been so alluring had turned to stone. Julie recoiled as if bitten by a snake. She felt strength drain from her body like water disappears down the kitchen sink. "Rose!" Somehow, she had to bring things back to reality, back to the way they were, back to the way they used to be when she had walked away from family and friends to go with this anointed and wonderful woman of God.

"Julie, it's no use. You have Jean now and…"

Julie tapped the back of her teaspoon on the table. "No, no you don't understand at all! God told me to help Jean, but that doesn't mean she has to spend the rest of her life with us. In fact, you're the one who mentioned we needed to help her, and Jean is a wonderful, moral, committed Christian. She wants to see you succeed and . . ."

"Julie, you know there's not enough room in that small motor home for all three of us, and remember, I never said she was welcome in *my* ministry. She's not ready for ministry anyway. You seem to forget that it's *my* call, *my* ministry, and I'm the president. I am asking you to write me your letter of resignation."

"What!" Julie countered, her voice tinged with hurt and anger. "You can't mean that! You said we were a team, that you couldn't do it without me." Her mind was racing. "After all I've done for you? After all the thousands and thousands of dollars I invested into this ministry? After I've practically laid down my life for you?" She felt as if she was going to faint. The room spun crazily around her. She pushed her hands down at her sides and onto the soft seat to steady herself.

"I'll pay for my coffee," Rose's tone was nonchalant. She began to rise from the booth. "I'll be coming to the motor home to retrieve the checkbook and my belongings."

"Before you leave," Julie's look halted Rose's progress, "May I remind you that you once promised me you'd never, *ever* do to me what Barbara Weston did to you!"

Rose's lips tightened into a thin line. She picked up her purse, gave Julie a warning look, and then said, "I'm sorry it has to be this way, Julie. We had a lot of good times together and a lot of laughs. But I simply cannot have anyone in my ministry I can't trust." Then, almost wistfully, she added, "I'll miss you, Julie." She turned and walked to the counter.

Julie remained in the booth for several minutes after Rose had exited the café. She felt weak and faint. But finally, she managed to stumble out into the brilliant sunshine. Her legs felt as if they were made of cement. She numbly walked back to the church where the RV was parked. The noticed the sign in front of the church which read: SPECIAL SPEAKER, EVANGELIST ROSE MILLER. COME AND BE BLESSED. ALL WELCOME.

Julie gasped as she stared at the sign. Suddenly an image overshadowed the bold announcement. Julie's heart hammered in her head as she watched the rose unfold, each petal delicately and perfectly placed around the intricate center; then she saw the curvature of the stem. Something was protruding from the image—yes, there it was! A single thorn. Julie watched, transfixed with horror, as the spiny appendage pierced a hand, a delicate hand like that of a woman. Blood oozed from the puncture. She traced its path from the gaping wound, down across the open palm until it finally vanished from sight into thick darkness.

# 27

# THE AXE TO THE ROOT

*For the Lord your God is he that goeth with you, to fight
for you against your enemies, to save you. - Deuteronomy 20:4*

Julie felt Pastor Manning's presence behind her as the service
began. She and Jean had tried to slip into the church unnoticed.
They silently brushed past the long table in the foyer, stacked with
Rose's "business" cards and Barbara Weston's books, and
slipped into the back pew.

Julie fought to control her churning emotions as the worship
service began. She wanted with all her heart for God to be exalted
in this place. She felt responsible for these meetings. After all, it
had been because of her and Jean's recommendation that Rose
was invited to minister. The least she could do, for the church's
sake, was to put aside her own problems and do what she could
to help.

*It's strange*, she told herself, *that Pastor Manning isn't sitting
up front where ministers usually sit.* She could feel his bright, gray
eyes boring into the back of her head. *Oh well, every pastor is
different* she thought.

The singing ended and Rose took her place behind the pulpit.
She lifted her arms, threw back her head and closed her eyes. As
the minutes ticked on, Julie heard Pastor Manning clear his throat.
Jean squirmed uncomfortably next to her. "What in the world is

Rose doing?" she whispered in her ear. Julie shrugged her shoulders in reply.

Finally, Rose's dramatic stance ended and she looked around the packed sanctuary. "I want to introduce my daughter, Donna, to you. She is going to sing, 'No More Night'."

Julie's mouth opened in surprise. She exchanged glances with Jean. "I didn't know she was here!" Julie whispered to Jean, keenly aware of the Pastor's continued scrutiny.

There was no doubt about it, Donna could sing. Then Rose, glowing triumphantly, stepped to the pulpit and preached a lengthy sermon about the secret place. *We've heard this message before.* Julie silently contemplated the familiar words. Suddenly, the pieces clicked into place in her memory. *This is a message Barbara Weston preached! The difference is,* Julie concluded, *Barbara had a real anointing on her. This is second-hand manna!*

Finally, it was over, and Julie and Jean moved to exit the church. But people, eager to look at the books on the table, blocked their way.

Julie felt a light tap on her shoulder. She turned to see Pastor Manning smiling down at her. "Julie," his voice was rich and kind, "Since you're all a team, can you please stay with the books and help out?"

"Oh, uh, of course." Julie stammered. She glanced over at Jean who nodded in agreement. "We'll take care of it together." Julie mentally reprimanded herself, *That was a stupid thing to say, dummy. You're pretending you're still a team, and now he'll suspect something's wrong.*

Julie and Jean were kept busy by a continual stream of people who wanted to purchase the books. "Barbara Weston is a famous author," Julie heard Jean tell a tall woman who was reading the back cover of one of Barbara's best-sellers. "You can make a check out to her and we'll forward it."

Julie smiled to herself. *That Jean sure catches on fast. Rose isn't going to like the idea of us contacting Barbara, but those books are on consignment. Besides, I want to speak with Barbara more than anything right now. I have plenty of questions to ask about Rose.*

"Excuse me, Julie. May I see you in my office?" Pastor Manning's gentle eyes searched her face. She cast a furtive glance over her shoulder at Jean. "Okay, I'll be right there. Jean can finish up here." She followed his stocky frame down the dimly-lit corridor.

"Have a seat, Julie." He motioned to a chair in front of his desk as he walked to the other side and sat down. He pursed his lips, folded his hands behind his head, tilted back in the swivel chair and looked at her for a long moment.

Julie studied the masculine contours of his face, the square jaw, the well-shaped nose, as if he were a model for one of her portraits. Pastor Manning cleared his throat and said abruptly, "Julie, something doesn't gel. There's something wrong." He leaned forward and folded his fingers on his desktop. Julie sat rigidly in the chair, praying silently for wisdom.

"Let me explain," he said, lifting his eyes to meet hers. "Martha and I have, time and time again, seen ministries in trouble. This one is no exception." Julie gulped, stared down at her white sandals and remained silent. He continued, "There's a breach. It goes like this—Rose and Donna on one side and you and Jean on the other. I also think you need to know I do not care for Rose's style, nor is there any anointing on that singer."

Julie's head was spinning. Had she heard correctly? Pastor Manning said matter-of-factly, "Martha and I believe you and Jean have true hearts of love for God, but I am sorry I ever booked Rose."

Julie's heart pounded so loudly in her own ears she was certain Pastor Manning could hear it thumping and banging in her chest. Tears escaped from under her closed eyelids and splashed noiselessly on her flowered blouse. She reached for a tissue, wiped her eyes and blew her nose. Pastor Manning wasn't through speaking. She looked up as he continued, "Julie, Martha and I can see right through all of this. We understand. Now, I want to let you know, we plan to let the meetings continue, but I will not write her a letter of recommendation or encourage other pastors to have her. As for you and Jean, we want you to consider ministering here in our church."

Julie looked up in disbelief. God was surely working in strange ways, but in her behalf. Still wounded by Rose's betrayal, but greatly encouraged by Pastor Manning's acceptance, she let him pray for her, thanked him, and slipped out of his office.

Jean looked up as Julie approached the table and grinned. Most of Barbara's books had been sold. Julie glanced around the room, searching for Rose. She was at the front of the church giving her "compassionate look" as one of the women poured out her heart to her. "Let's get out of here," Julie whispered to Jean. "I've got lots to tell you!"

Settled comfortably in the privacy of the motor home, Julie and Jean faced each other over two cups of coffee. "Wow," Jean said after Julie related Pastor Manning's conversation with her. "Well, praise the Lord, Julie. He knows all things; He tries the hearts and the reins. He brought us here for more reasons than one."

Julie looked into the thoughtful, hazel eyes. *Yes,* her mind agreed, *God hasn't forsaken me. He not only used me to help Jean through her tough time, but He raised her up to go through this horrible time with me.* She smiled in spite of the turmoil in her heart. "Yes, I'm beginning to see how right you are!" Julie acknowledged that she would have been destroyed if God hadn't sent Jean with her. Now, rather than being the strong one for Jean, Jean was the pillar she could lean on until she got through the worst of the storm.

That night Julie dreamed of two trees. Their trunks weren't large, but rather than growing straight and independently as trees should, they were grotesquely intertwined. Then an axe appeared. Julie watched as it struck a blow to the base of the trees. Slowly the twisted trunks gave way with a groan. Then the insatiable axe, unsatisfied with its victory, cut deeper still. Down, down, down it went, hacking and chopping until every vestige of root was destroyed.

Julie bolted straight up in bed, shaking and sobbing. Instantly Jean was at her side, praying for her friend. "It's Him!" Julie managed to choke out the words. "It's God! He's cutting down the root. It wasn't right! It was a horrible, ugly soul tie." Jean's eyes widened as Julie poured out her anguish. "I allowed her and her ministry to come before Christ." She folded her arms across her abdomen. "Oh, it hurts! It hurts so very much! I don't know what to do...so far from home...I'll never trust anyone again. Not ever! Oh! It's so painful!"

"I know, Julie, I know." Jean's tone was reassuring, calm. "We will pray through all of this; you and me together. Trust the Lord with your life, Julie. He's the only One you can lean on. He will heal and hold your heart, I know. And," Jean added with conviction, "God has put us together. We're in the same boat, but we're not alone. The Master of the sea, and the wind, is in the boat with us!"

# 28

# THE DISAPPEARANCE

*Give heed to me, O Lord, and hearken to the voice*
*of them that contend with me. - Jeremiah 18:19*

Three weeks after the meetings in Flagstaff at Brother Manning's church, Julie and Jean found themselves in Phoenix. They reflected on Pastor Manning and his charming wife, who had been discerning, supportive, and honest. Julie and Jean rejoiced in the fact that they had been invited to return in two months to hold meetings of their own.

Palm trees swayed gently in the balmy night air, and the usual roar of traffic on Phoenix's main streets dulled to an occasional burst of noise. Julie and Jean strolled together down a well-lit boulevard, enjoying this rare opportunity to relax. "I'm sorry you have to go through this miserable phase of the journey," Julie said. "I mean, having to park the RV in Harrison's yard while Rose gets the plush guest room in their house. They are so rude, locking us out so we are forced to use the restrooms at Denny's because the RV holding tanks are full."

"Well, I'm glad I'm here," Jean said thoughtfully. "But I feel badly for you. This whole thing is the pits. I mean, trying to negotiate through everything with Rose while the Harrisons act as mediators. Just to think that all this is just because they were instrumental in getting Rose ordained through their phony organization and getting her that non-profit status!  Now to think of their nerve in trying to get you to turn over every cent to Rose! Who do they think they are? Don't they understand whatever money came in to the ministry was mostly from your friends and your art work?" Jean kicked disgustedly at a small rock in front of her.

Julie watched it skitter down the walkway. "They are totally sucked in," she looked up at the twinkling stars, "just like I was."

"That was a horrible scene the other night," Jean's voice rang with disgust. "I mean, when Rose threw a fit because you insisted you were going to keep your post office box up in Kalispell."

"It really was bad, wasn't it?" Julie agreed. "She's stripped me of everything, but since I'm paying the rent up there and since that's the only home I have, I'm not about to give up the post office box.  Besides," her voice betrayed her irritation, "She's in Arizona most of the time. She's just afraid she might get mail up there and I won't forward it to her."

"Also," Jean added, "Remember, she insures her car up there because insurance rates are cheaper than in Phoenix."

"Well, now that they have your letter of resignation, all we have to do is get Rose to pay for all those long-distance calls she made to Melody over the past three months or so, right?"

Julie sighed. "You're right. That's quite a bill! I wonder what she and Melody talked about all the time? Probably us!" She grimaced. "But where in the world is she? I haven't seen her around the place for two days. The other meetings we set up don't begin for three more weeks. Hey, I've got an idea," she said brightly, "Let's call her kids tomorrow and see if they've seen her, okay?"

"That's a good idea.  If we can get all the loose ends tied up, then we can leave and head back toward Flagstaff." Jean halted abruptly, shoved her hands in her jean pockets, and faced Julie. "Something's up. I can feel it. But I'm not sure what."

A knot formed in Julie's stomach. "Yeah, I sense foul play too. Come on, let's go back and pray for God's direction."

Early the following morning the women walked to Denny's Restaurant to use the pay phone. Julie dialed Donna's number. Ralph's voice could be heard on a phone recorder, "...leave a message after the beep." Julie hesitated, then hung up. What good would it do to leave a message? Rose undoubtedly wouldn't return her call and leave a message with the Harrisons. She felt anger rising within her. Rose had no business using her calling card and making all those long-distance calls. *And to think she wanted her name on my gas credit card,* Julie thought. *Thank God I didn't fall for that one or I'd never dig myself out of this financial pit.*

"I'll just call Duane," she muttered to Jean. "He surely will know where his mother is." Julie mentally counted the rings. *One, two, three, four, five...oh Duane, get up!*

"Hullo?" Duane's muffled voice was music to her ears. "Duane? This is Julie. I must speak to your mother. Where is she?" There was a long silence. "Duane, can you hear me, where's...?"

"I dunno." Duane's tone suddenly became wary, "I think she's with Donna." The phone clicked in her ear.

"Okay," Julie said with new resolve. "Here goes." She dialed Debbie's number and waited. "Good morning!" Debbie's voice rang good naturedly.

"Hi, Deb, this is Julie and I absolutely must find Rose. Do you know..."

Debbie cut in abruptly, "No, Julie, I'm sorry but I haven't the faintest idea where she is. I haven't seen her in days. I've got to run. Bye." Click.

Jean clamped her lips together as if to say, "'Something stinks in Denmark.'" Julie's frustration showed in her tear-filled eyes. "What on earth is she up to, Jean?"

"I don't know, but she's got to be up to something! Why don't we treat ourselves to a cheap breakfast while we're here and think about what we should do next."

"Great idea!" Julie responded.

By the time the two friends had finished breakfast, Julie's nerves had settled. "Hey, Jean! I have an idea. Let's call Patsy!"

"Okay. She needs to know what's happening anyway."

Fumbling for her phone calling card, Julie bounced back to the pay phone. If anyone on this earth could cheer Julie, it would be Patsy. Julie believed that even if heaven and earth passed away, Patsy and Daniel would always be her friends. With trembling fingers, Julie dialed the familiar number.

"Hello?" Julie could have jumped for joy. "Patsy? How are you? Boy do I ever miss you!"

"Julie, is that really you?" Patsy's surprised voice rang loudly over the phone. "What's up? How are the meetings going?" Then she added before Julie could respond, "You sound funny."

"I've got so much to tell you! Jean and I have been going through some horrible things, but God is with us and . . ."

"Where's Rose?" Patsy's voice sounded strangely distant. Something inside of Julie sounded an alarm, but Julie pushed past it.

"Well, that's just it. I hate to tell you this, but I was wrong, I mean, about Rose. It's a long story, but to make it short, let's just say the woman is a phony and a leach. She waited until I ran out of money and then dumped me . . ."

"Stop!" Patsy's scream halted Julie's unwise explanation of events. "Stop! I don't believe you, Julie. I want to hear Rose's side of this!"

Julie was stunned. Her throat constricted into a knot, and prickles of sweat broke out over her limp body. "Patsy, listen," she said weakly, as Jean, who had been listening to Julie's side of the conversation, moved closer to the receiver.

"No, Julie. I don't want to hear it. I know what I feel about Rose. You are wrong. Let's just leave it at that. I will always love you, Julie, but I think it's best if we just stay away from each other." The receiver banged mercilessly in Julie's ear.

"I just can't believe it!" Julie dropped into a nearby folding chair. "I just can't believe Patsy would do this to me. I'm the one who led her and Daniel to the Lord! I've always loved them with all my heart. I just can't believe it!" Tears flowed unchecked down her cheeks.

Jean knew Julie was totally overwhelmed with shock and sorrow. She pulled a chair up next to her friend. "This same thing has happened to me many times, Julie. Of all the young people I introduced to Jesus and discipled, not one has even bothered to find out where I am or how I am. That's the way people are. We serve God because we love Him, not because of the way people treat us—one way or the other."

"I'm sorry, Jean. I hate self-pity, but I just don't think I can take much more."

"Let's go on back to the RV and see if anything came for us in the mail today," Jean said thoughtfully. "Perhaps someone has sent some cheer our way in care of the Harrisons."

When the girls returned to the motor home, they found an envelope stuffed in the door. "Aha!" Julie exclaimed, trying to sound cheerful in spite of an aching heart. "You were right! A letter from Nolene Davis! I wonder what she has to say?" She eagerly tore open the envelope. Her eyes widened in horror. She tore open the door, stomped into the RV and threw herself onto the narrow couch. Startled, Jean followed her frustrated and anguished friend.

"What on earth did she say?" Jean quizzed. She snatched up the crumpled letter from the table where Julie had tossed it and quickly scanned its contents. "Oh no!"

"I am so mad!" Julie stormed. "How could she do this to me?"

Jean slowly read the letter out loud, as if she, too, couldn't believe what Nolene had written. "Dear Julie and Jean, I hope this letter finds you. I think you should know that Rose is up here. She flew up, and she and Melody have been out at the house going through everything. One day Rose had me go with her to verify what she took, but I had no way of knowing what was yours and what was hers. She moved it over to Melody's place. It looks like she will be spending time here with Melody and won't keep the house. So, at least you'll still have a place to live. She told us Jean took over her ministry. We're confused, but we love you. I know you'll explain later. We're praying for you. Love, Nolene and Hank."

"So," Julie looked up at Jean who stood in disbelief, staring at the letter, "So now we know why she disappeared. I wonder just how much of my stuff has also vanished."

# 29

# UNDERSTANDING IMAGES

*And ye shall know the truth, and the*
*truth shall make you free. - John 8:32*

The scheduled meetings in Flagstaff at Pastor Manning's church went well. Julie was impressed with Jean's willingness to serve the Lord in any capacity. She proved to be an able minister and teacher, and the people loved her. Truly, the Holy Spirit had thoroughly discipled her in the things of God.

As they prepared to return to Montana, fear and dread overshadowed Julie's heart. What would she find once she stepped inside the door? With every passing day Julie grew more thankful to God that He had foreseen what she called her "holocaust" and had put Jean in her life.

Exhausted but wiser, Julie and Jean pulled out of Flagstaff, after bidding their new friends "good-bye," and headed north. As the miles melted beneath them, Julie and Jean enjoyed reliving the services they had held. Many people had responded to the moving and ministry of the Holy Spirit, and both Julie and Jean rejoiced. Jesus had clearly been lifted up and glorified.

As they neared Reno, Jean, who was at the wheel, pulled into the parking lot of a small café. "Time for a well-deserved break," she said. They stiffly exited the RV and walked into the friendly atmosphere of the nearly empty room. Finding a corner table, they dropped into the cushioned seats and waited for the waitress.

"Hi, girls," the congenial waitress greeted them with a smile. "What can I get for you?" They ordered iced tea and two hamburgers.

"Julie," Jean smiled, "I really want to go over the nature information with you again."

"Ah, Jean," Julie sighed wearily, "Can it wait? I really don't get it. Besides, I'm not sure if it's biblical or not. And, if it isn't, then I'm just not buying it."

"Okay," Jean responded cautiously, "Let me prove to you it's biblical and that it bears good fruit. You're the type that needs proof!"

Julie looked at her sharply. That was one thing Jean had right.

Then as Jean began to share with her what the Lord had revealed about people's natures, certain things became clear which before had been shrouded in uncertainty. "Julie, believe me," Jean's tone was dead serious, "I'm telling you what God showed me about people." Julie shifted uncomfortably in her chair. Even though she could agree with some things, Jean was beginning to grate on Julie's nerves. But Jean had a captive audience, and she wouldn't let up.

"Julie, listen! God is a God of total, absolute, complete order. He created four natures of people. The number four, which corresponds with the Hebrew alphabet, is the Universal Number which pertains to the earth and everything to do with the things of the earth."

Julie swallowed a bite of her hamburger, sighed and dabbed at the corner of her mouth with her napkin. Jean continued, "You know, like the four seasons, the four corners of the earth, the four cups at Passover, there are the four-footed beasts, four sides to the Tabernacle, four gospels, and so on. Everything that has to do with the material creation on earth is *four*." Jean eyed Julie apprehensively. Julie smiled weakly, trying to show her friendship to Jean was real but her acceptance of this theory of hers wasn't. Encouraged, Jean continued, "God showed me this information after working with all those young people in Big Fork. I asked Him a couple of questions about why some people go through terrible trials while others seemingly don't. He showed me it was their process. Then I felt prompted to ask Him what determined their process, and He told me it depended on their form of rebellion."

Julie felt her stomach form into a tight knot. She sipped her iced tea and looked out the window. Couldn't Jean take a hint? She didn't believe it and she didn't want to hear it, *again!*

"Take for example," Jean was on a roll and Julie knew it, "That husband of yours." Julie's ears perked up. Perhaps this part would be worth listening to. "Yeah?" she responded.

Jean's lips formed a crooked smile. "Gary! Both he and my husband, Jack, are what is called self-assured." She surveyed Julie's skeptical face for a moment, but pursued the subject like a blood hound on the scent of a rabbit. "This nature has an image in front of them all the time. According to what you've told me about Gary, in public he always had a 'good guy' image, but behind closed doors he was a tyrant." Julie nodded in agreement. Finally, something made sense about all this nature stuff. "Well," Jean said slowly, as if hoping each word would somehow sink in, "Jack was the same nature and he had the same image. That's why I married him. I fell for that image."

Julie's eyes widened. This is exactly what had happened to her! What else was Jean saying? Oh yes, something about a list. "Self-assured people are perfectionists because of their standards and lists. In other words, they have these high standards they are trying to live up to because of their images. They have different images, too. For example, they have one image as a Christian, another as an employee, another as a husband and another as a son or a father and so on. As for the women, they have an image

170

as a woman, as a wife, mother, or daughter. Get it? Now, here's the part that's tough! They also have standards and images for others. For example, Gary had an image for you, Julie. And if you didn't measure up to it twenty-four hours a day, then he'd put it on his *list*."

Julie was hooked. Nobody had ever explained Gary's strange behavior to her until now. Gary had actually shown her a written list against his ex-wife. He kept it in his billfold on a little slip of paper. Now she knew how he justified his actions toward her. He had a list against her, too, and, whenever they got in a fight, he would bring up that stupid, petty list! She begged Jean for more information. And she got it.

Jean smiled confidently. "Okay, here goes Julie. Each nature has its own wall of protection, fear, and need. What motivates people is having their needs met. Self-assured natured people need recognition for what they are trying to become. Your nature needs emotional love. That's what you were trying to get from Gary."

Julie leaned forward. This was the most interesting thing she had ever heard. And so far, it was all true. "You need lots of proof," Jean said as she wiped her fingers on her napkin. She sipped her iced tea. "That's why I've tried to prove this is from the Lord. You fear rejection."

Suddenly Julie's jumble of confusion evaporated. It was, as she later testified, "as if the light came on." She nearly dropped her glass of iced tea in her excitement. "Yes! I get it! I see what happened!" Jean leaned back in her chair and watched as Julie's entire demeanor became transformed by truth. "I was vulnerable, really vulnerable when I met Rose, and she knew it!" Julie's eyes widened and she slapped the top of the table with her open palm. "Jean!" The people in the far end of the café stopped eating and conversing to stare in Julie's direction.

"Jean," she repeated, this time lowering her voice, "Rose is self-assured by nature, isn't she? And I bought that beguiling image, hook, line, and sinker! What a sucker I was."

Jean grinned. "No, my friend, you weren't a sucker, but you sure did take the bait. But how would you have known any different? You were beguiled by her image, and probably a spirit of seduction."

"Expensive education," Julie growled. She sat for a moment staring into space. It all made perfectly good sense now. Rose even had her stupid, petty list of lies against Julie so she could justify her actions. "Man, Jean. Rose didn't even so much as tell me 'Thank you' for all I did. All that money," she paused, and then finished in a word, "Gone!"

"Well, let me tell you some of the people in the Bible who were self-assured," Jean said as she nodded 'yes' to the waitress who hovered over them with a pitcher of iced tea. "There was Adam, who had the image of God, and Cain, Moses, Job, King Saul, and Judas Iscariot."

"Wow!" Julie exclaimed excitedly. "Knowing this is going to make Bible study even more interesting! What about the other three natures? What are they?"

"There is the submissive, which is what I am. You know, the analytical type. I have to analyze everything before coming to a conclusion." She giggled. "Quite the opposite of impulsive you!"

Julie laughed. "You've really got my number all right."

"Then there are the strong-willed people, like your mother. This nature is more widely understood. These people fear losing control, they draw their own lines, and they are extreme in whatever they do. Their greatest need is respect."

"Barbara Weston!" Julie exclaimed. "She's very black and white and, speaking of Barbara, I can't wait until we talk to her! I'm so glad I still have her home address. She should be returning from Africa in a couple of months, if I remember correctly."

"Let me give you some examples from scripture of your nature." It was obvious to Julie that Jean was in her element. Sharing information was what she loved to do. "There was curious Eve, doubtful Gideon, emotional King David, the weeping prophet, Jeremiah, Nehemiah, doubting Thomas, and the Apostle Peter. All emotional, all needing proof, all with big hearts." Jean yawned and stretched.

"Before we leave," Julie leaned forward eagerly, "Can you quickly tell me who some of the strong-willed people were?"

"Sure," Jean said as she picked up her purse. "Let me see, there was Joseph, Jacob's son, Jezebel, the prophetess Deborah, Jonah, and the Apostle Paul, to name a few. And, I suppose," she added with a grin of satisfaction, "You'd like to know who was submissive?"

Julie nodded. Now that her imagination was piqued, she had to know the rest.

"Mary, the mother of Jesus, Isaiah, Daniel the prophet, and the Apostle John."

"Wow," Julie said in a hushed voice.

"Hey, Julie!" Jean coaxed. "Let's go. We have a long way to travel before it gets dark."

# 30

# VIOLATED

*Fearfulness and trembling are come upon me,*
*and horror hath overwhelmed me. - Psalm 55:5*

The sound of gravel crunching under the RV's tires woke Julie. She glanced over at Jean as she slowed to a stop. "Home?" Julie asked, suddenly wide awake.

"Yep. We're finally here." Jean pulled on the parking brake, turned off the headlights and looked at Julie. "This is it."

"Well, we might as well get it over with," Julie said. She dreaded going into the house. What if Rose took everything? How would she get it back?

The girls exited the cab and made their way to the front door. The yard light illuminated the driveway, yard, and front of the house, making it easier for them to see. The sound of crickets and a hoot owl gave evidence that there was still some form of life on the otherwise seemingly abandoned farm.

Julie fumbled in her purse for the house key. "Here it is," she said, "And here we go." She turned the lock and pushed on the door. Stepping inside, she flipped on the light switch. "What on earth...?" Julie exclaimed. "Melody and Rose must have left the back door ajar." She hurried across the living room and into the kitchen.

A fine film of black top soil coated the floors, walls, windows, curtains, and furniture. The wind-blown black dirt from the neighbor's plowed field lay in drifts along the window sills and hung from spider webs. Julie's brown eyes filled with tears. "I just want to scream!" she shrieked in frustration. "Rose took the desk, the file cabinet, and my sewing machine!"

"Hey, Julie, come here!" Jean called from the living room. "They left a note for you on the end table." She held it out for Julie.

Julie took the yellow paper from Jean. It read, "I have taken what belonged to me. I am keeping the computer and printer since I have to finish my book. Nolene was here to witness that I only took what was mine. You can have the. TV, the pots and pans, and dishes. I am keeping the sound equipment and microphone because I need it for my ministry. Rose."

"The nerve! It just so happens I bought that TV, and the sound equipment, and the other things were mine in the first place!" Julie stormed into her bedroom. "She even took my quilt!"

"Did you ever let her use it?" Jean asked.

"Well, yes, but what does that have to do with it?" Julie questioned.

"Self-assured people assume that once they use something, then it belongs to them," Jean explained in a hushed voice. "Come on, Julie, let's sleep out in the motor home one more night. We're both exhausted, and well, it's a sure thing we can't stay in here!" She looked around at the film of dirt. "I'll get busy and clean it up in the morning."

Julie slept fitfully. Tossing and turning, a jumble of thoughts assailed her weary mind. *Well, Julie, you are reaping what you sowed. You should've listened to your mother and Ruth.* Julie moaned in her sleep. The accusations continued to hammer against her. *Do you realize you literally lost a new home and all the furnishings for that Rose? Do you know what a fool you look like? Do you realize that now you're nearly poverty-stricken?* Julie's eyes fluttered open as the words marched triumphantly around her mind like enemy soldiers circling a fortified city. *You reap what you sow... you reap what you sow... you reap what you sow.*

Julie pressed her hands against the sides of her head. The wind howled and shook their little shelter on wheels, rocking it violently. The darkness of the night seemed thick and heavy. Great, wracking sobs tore at her body. Something within her snapped and she caved in to the hopelessness and sorrow she had carried for months.

Jean, a light sleeper, jumped off of her cramped sleeping quarters. "Julie, Julie! What's going on?" She fumbled for the light switch. The battery-powered light flickered on, barely illuminating Julie's trembling form huddled in the corner. "No, no no!" Julie stammered between sobs. "I quit! God knows, I can't handle this. I can't go on like this anymore. I can't go back into that house. Never! Never!"

Jean's concern showed in her voice. "Julie! Stop it! I'm here; you're not alone. We can face this with the Lord's help. He's here with us!"

"No! He doesn't care! He's angry with me! Don't you see? I wasted it all! I wasted everything! I'm a fool!"

"Julie, that's not true!" Jean put her hands on Julie's shoulders and gently shook her. "Snap out of it, Julie! God loves you."

"No! No, He doesn't! He doesn't have to love a stupid fool like me!" Julie's voice rose hysterically.

"Julie!" Jean's voice was commanding. "What does the Bible say? Tell me what the Bible says! Now!"

Julie lapsed into a sullen silence. Her body continued to be wracked by sobs. "Oh, Julie," Jean continued to fight for her friend, "Jesus loves you. He knows you just wanted to serve Him. God looks at the heart! You have a pure heart, and that's what counts!"

"Then, why did He let this happen to me? Why?" Julie screamed defiantly.

"Because God is preparing you for a greater anointing, for greater ministry. Remember Romans 8:28?"

Julie nodded numbly. "Yeah. I know."

"Say it! Right now! Out loud!" Jean demanded.

"'And we know that all things work together for good to them that love God, to them who are the called according to his purpose'."

Jean leaned closer to Julie and peered into her face. The Word of God was having its effect. At least she had quit crying uncontrollably. "All right then, would you like a cup of herb tea and some time together? We can take all this to the Lord."

"Yes, I'd like that," Julie said meekly. For the next hour Jean gently ministered God's truths to Julie until she relaxed enough to go back to sleep.

Morning dawned bright and clear, although the wind was still blowing hard. Jean and Julie faced the overwhelming chore of cleaning the dirt out of the house. "It just doesn't seem fair, somehow," Julie muttered as she tried to wash off the kitchen counter, "To have to come home after all we've been through, thoroughly exhausted, and then have to tackle this horrendous mess!" The wet sponge instantly turned the fine, black top soil into mud. "Ugh!" She called to Jean who was busy vacuuming the living room. "How on earth are we ever going to get all this dirt cleaned up when we can't even use water?"

"We'll just have to keep sweeping, vacuuming, shaking, and dusting!" Jean declared. "Julie, why don't you start bringing our things in from the motor home, and I'll clean the house."

As Julie threw herself into the task of unloading their belongings, she began to feel somewhat as if she were accomplishing something. She carried some of Jean's clothes up to her bedroom and decided to step into her art studio to appraise the condition of the sun-lit room. Suddenly, her eyes widened in horror. Scattered around the room were dozens of photographs.

Her photo book lay open, and Julie could see many of the pictures were missing. "Rose!" she screamed, "How could you!" Someone had gone through Julie's photo albums, taking out certain pictures and leaving others. "It was my camera, my film." Julie began to realize it could take weeks, or even months, for her to fully discover just what Rose had helped herself to.

Jean's attack on the house was paying off. Soon enough of a trail had been blazed through the dirt to make the place functional. By the following day, Julie worked up enough courage to place a phone call to Melody. She had a list of things which she was determined to recover, including her computer.

Melody's cheerful voice answered the phone, "Hello?"

"Hi, Melody. How are you? This is Julie." There was an uncomfortable pause on the other end of the line.

"Oh, hello." She waited.

Julie decided to get right to the point. "Rose came through the house and took some of my things. I need to come over and get them back."

"Oh, really? Well, I went with her several times to the house, and she only took what was hers."

Julie felt her temperature rising. How on earth could Melody know what belonged to Rose? She only knew what Rose told her! "Well, I'm coming over and I want my computer."

"I'm sorry, Julie, but it won't do you any good." Melody said firmly, "Rose stored her things here, and unless I get her say so, I can't let you have them."

Julie's voice rose uncontrollably, "Listen, Melody. I worked four different jobs in Phoenix to support Rose and pay for that computer!" She heard Melody snicker. So that was it, they had their little conspiracy. That certainly accounted for the high telephone bill.

"You can call Rose at Donna's," Melody advised, "And if she wants to give you anything, then she can call and let me know."

Jean motioned for Julie to hang up. "I've got to go. Good-bye," Julie said in an even tone.

"Let it go, Julie. Just let her have the stuff," Jean's hazel eyes registered her disgust with Rose.

"No, Jean. You don't understand. I about killed myself working all the time to pay off the stuff she just had to have. And, I was sick most of that time to boot. I can't just let her waltz off with it." Julie paced back and forth angrily. "Besides, we need it for our ministry. All we have now is one old typewriter between us."

"Let her have it, Julie," Jean repeated. "God will provide for us. She won't give it to you anyway, and to force the issue will just make a bad scene. Do you want to put a reproach on the Gospel in this small community?"

"Well, no, of course not." Julie knew she had lost. But how much more did she have to lose? Everything, it seemed, was going down the drain. She knew her mother had disinherited her on top of it all. She had lost Patsy and Daniel, people she loved deeply. She had lost much of her health and all of her money. It wasn't going to be easy for her and Jean to make a go of it. Jobs were scarce in this part of the country. On top of that, God was saying "No" every time they prayed and asked Him if He wanted them to look for work.

As if reading her thoughts, Jean smiled and said, "Faith. Now we're really learning what it means to live by faith!"

A few days later, Jean and Julie decided to go into Kalispell to shop. Jean put on her jacket and was heading for the door when she noticed Julie huddled on a chair in the corner. "Julie, wha-a-a-a—"

"No! I can't go! I can't leave the house. I can't do it!" Julie was shaking and crying.

Quickly summing up the situation, Jean walked over to her friend. "It's Rose, isn't it? You're afraid of the same thing happening all over again, aren't you?" By this time Julie was nearly hysterical. "Julie, Rose is clear down in Arizona for all we know. It'll be okay, believe me!"

"No, no, no!" Julie's eyes were wide with fear. She couldn't explain what was happening to her, but whatever it was, it was real.

"Okay, Julie," her wise friend confided, "It's like this. You feel betrayed, violated, raped." She waited for Julie's response.

"Yes!" she screamed. "Rape, it's like being defiled, exposed, violated. Yes! That explains it. I can't leave, never." She, pulled up her knees, wrapped her arms around them, dropped her head, and sat in a tight little huddle.

"Julie, listen to me. You can't sit in this house forever! It's okay. I understand, but the Lord has given this house to you to live in. He even forced Melody to sell it to her brother while we were in Arizona, so we pay rent to him, and you don't even have to pay rent to her anymore. Think of it, how God has intervened. This place is God's place, Julie, and Rose isn't going to ransack it again. It's okay," she coaxed. "Let's pray about this right now." She walked over to Julie and began praying for her.

Julie began to unwind. Finally, she consented to go into town. "Let's change the lock, okay? Get new keys and everything."

"Sure," Jean answered, "That's a great idea. We'll both feel better."

"Let's treat ourselves to pizza while we're there." Julie had finally snapped out of it.

Jean's lips formed a crooked smile. "You bet, partner. We'll make a day of it."

# 31

# THE ROSE UNVEILED

*I AM the rose of Sharon. - Song of Solomon 2:1*

Julie deftly rolled pie dough between two pieces of waxed paper for a rhubarb pie, placed it in the pan, and scooped in the filling. Everything had to be "just right" for the visiting evangelist.

Jean had busied herself with last minute cleaning and polishing. Flowers freshly cut that morning, added colorful beauty to the cozy living room. Both girls thanked God for this opportunity to fellowship with the very woman who not only would be able to answer many of their questions about Rose, but also help in other spiritual matters.

As it was, Julie had perceptibly changed. There was a spiritual depth and certain sobriety which had been lacking before. She could literally feel the changes which had taken place in her heart. Julie knew God had allowed everything which had happened to her in the past, including the tumultuous and costly situation with Rose. Her struggles to fully comprehend why her life seemed to be one long string of disappointment and rejection was now clear. The cross of Christ. That was the answer.

Julie admitted she had shifted her gaze from Christ's sufficiency to others: husband, friends, church, pastors, and even ministry. Now she knew with every fiber of her being that she must never allow anything, or anyone, to ever deflect, mar, distract, or dim her relationship and dependency on the Son of God. Anything less than this was idolatry. Only Jesus satisfies. Only Jesus.

As Julie placed the "soon-to-be-golden-treasure-of-eating-pleasure," as she called it, into the waiting oven, Jean called excitedly from the front room. "She's here! Julie! Barbara's here!" Jean went flying out the front door to greet the smiling, but somewhat tired, evangelist.

Soon Barbara was comfortably settled in the sun-filled living room. She cradled Dede, her tiny black and tan dog, in her arms and grinned at Julie. "My, but life can take some strange turns, can't it?" Dede's devoted eyes scanned her owner's face as if trying to read her mind. Satisfied that Barbara wasn't going to move for a while, Dede curled up into a ball, sighed contentedly and fell asleep on her lap.

Julie's gaze momentarily wandered to the scenic Montana view framed by the large window behind the couch where her guest relaxed. Winter's starkness had slowly given way to softer shades of brilliant green as the deciduous trees faithfully sought to prove, once again, that life overcomes death. Not to be outdone, emerald blades of grass forced their way up through the brown sod. Yes, it was truly a time for new life.

"Here's our coffee," Jean announced as she entered the living room with a tray full of cups, napkins, sugar, cream, and spoons. "The pie should be out of the oven soon."

Barbara laughed. "Well, thank you! You girls didn't have to go to all this trouble, you know. I'm just thankful Dede and I have a place to stay during the revival meetings." She carefully measured the cream and sugar, stirring slowly as if not wishing to disturb her sleeping friend. "So, tell me, how are you girls doing out here?"

Julie leaned forward in her chair, cupping the pink and blue mug in her hand. Her long red hair was pulled up at the sides, held fast by a bright green bow, then cascaded down her back. Her eyes sparkled with life and her pink cheeks glowed. "We're doing good, praise the Lord. He is meeting our needs on a daily basis." She sipped her coffee and changed the subject. "We are so glad you're here and so eager to ask you a few questions, too!"

Barbara chuckled. "I expected as much." She stroked Dede's soft fur. "It's about Rose, right?"

Jean and Julie nodded in unison. "What is it about her, I mean, we know some things, but we want to hear what you have to say."

"Girls, Rose has a beguiling spirit. And it's big. You're not the first one to fall for it." She looked understandingly at Julie and went on, "I fell for it myself. But," she held up a finger, "Not for long. As soon as she left her husband and kids, she crawled into my life. Before I knew what was happening, she had completely taken control."

"Control?" Julie asked. "She accused *me* of having a spirit of control!"

Barbara laughed. "I know, I know. I had the same thing thrown at me. But, you know," she suddenly sobered, "Rose nearly destroyed my ministry. She ruined many friendships I had through the years with pastors and others. She literally took over my life! I lost two good cars because of her, and then she had the nerve to ask me to put her name on my bank account, travel trailer, and little home. She wanted it all!"

Barbara set her cup on a coaster, glanced down at Dede, and then looked straight into Julie's inquisitive eyes. Julie recalled the first time she had ever seen Barbara Weston. It seemed as if centuries had passed since that initial meeting in Dayport. Her memory stirred and suddenly released a forgotten incident. When Barbara had risen and moved up to the speaker's platform, the Holy Spirit within Julie had stood up. She didn't quite know how to describe it, but she had felt it happen. She had known then that Barbara was a true servant of God. This fact now gave support and credence to what she was about to hear.

"Julie, I will tell you about Rose. If I had known long ago that she would be coming into your life, I would have tried to warn you. But then," she said thoughtfully, "you wouldn't have received it at that time. Anyway," she continued, "when I first met Rose, she followed me everywhere. I tried to counsel her to stay at home and be a wife and mother. It was to no avail. Then one night she came to my place. She was hysterical. I had no choice but to take her in. One thing led to another, and against my better judgment, she persuaded me that I needed a traveling companion. I knew that she wanted to serve the Lord, but somehow things just never worked out."

"Yeah," Julie said slowly, "Rose told us about the night her husband was going to kill her and she got a gun and..."

"Bah!" Barbara interrupted. "She told you that story, too? Let me tell you, she never had a gun; I did. She was living with me and he came over to my place, and I was the one with the gun. Rose didn't like guns. In fact, she was terrified of them."

Jean and Julie exchanged looks. Julie got up to take the pie out of the oven and quickly returned to the living room. In some ways it made her feel better to think that a seasoned Christian like Evangelist Weston could be duped by Rose, too.

Barbara smiled and said softly, "You girls need to know that many of the stories Rose has told people, you know, the things she's writing a book about, never happened."

Julie gasped and Jean's eyes widened. "You mean," stammered Julie, "That I spent all that time, energy, and money for her to write a biography that's not true?"

Barbara nodded. "I'm afraid so. Even her family members verify that many of those sad stories are only a figment of her imagination."

Jean pursed her lips. "I can see how that can happen to a person with her nature," she said thoughtfully. "Some self-assured people are so deluded that they begin to believe what they imagine is actual fact."

"Very interesting," Barbara replied with a slight chuckle. "That explains a lot of things."

"I want to tell you what else has happened," Julie said as she stirred in her chair. "Rose cost me many friends. And my mother was so angry she disinherited me! But, praise the Lord, Noelene and Hank are still our friends." Julie glanced over at Jean and continued, "She told everybody we know that Jean came along and ruined her ministry—that Jean split us up! The truth is if it hadn't been for the Lord sending Jean into my life when He did, I would've ended up in the insane asylum my mother had a vivid dream about! So, in other words, Jean is the scapegoat."

"You've got to be kidding!" Barbara exclaimed, and then quickly added, "But, of course you're not! That is how she works. She justifies everything she does." A note of warning sounded in her voice, "And, I suspect there is a familiar spirit there too."

"What do you mean?" Jean leaned forward. This was something she wanted to know more about.

"Well, let me explain," Barbara said solemnly. "A familiar spirit familiarizes itself with someone and then tells that information to the person through whom it operates. Let me give you an example of how it works. Suppose you're talking about a person who operates with a familiar spirit. The familiar spirit will stir them up by giving them partial information about what has been said, and then they will act based on that information. People with a familiar spirit think their supernatural insights come from the Holy Spirit. That's why God warns us to test the spirits to see if they are from God."

The three friends sat for long moments in reflective silence. Finally, Barbara spoke up. "Let me tell you how she nearly ruined my ministry." Barbara's blue eyes reflected sorrow. "Everywhere we went Rose always 'saw' something. She either 'saw' that the pastor was having an affair, or that he abused his wife and kids, or else he was gay."

"What?" Jean said. "You're kidding!"

Barbara shook her head. "No, I'm afraid I'm dead serious. She always saw something wrong. At first, I trusted her so-called insights. Later, I realized that although she may have been right once in a while, she wasn't right all of the time. I lost many friends during those years and many valuable contacts."

While Jean poured another round of coffee, Julie thoughtfully said, "I remember now. She told me the same thing about a lot of ministers, too. In fact, that explains why she wouldn't accept meetings with certain pastors I contacted. I never understood it. I mean, it's hard enough to book meetings without being so picky and choosy. I used to think she had super discernment and wished I had it, too. It never once occurred to me she may have been wrong! In fact, I thought she was right all of the time. And, yes, she did tell Patsy and I that her husband, Bob, tried to kill her and *after* that she met you!"

"That explains her obsession with her grown children," Jean said slowly. "Guilt. She actually left them for her own selfish reasons, and now she overcompensates because of guilt!"

"Right!" Barbara agreed. "You've got it!"

Julie rose, disappeared into the kitchen and returned with steaming pieces of pie. "Wow, does that ever look good. Rhubarb is my favorite!" Barbara smiled.

They all ate for a few moments in silence, each lost in her own thoughts. Finally, Barbara looked at Julie. "Julie," Barbara's eyes held Julie's in an earnest grasp. Their depths mirrored an eternity of spiritual experience and wisdom, agony, and ecstasy, but most of all, knowledge of Him whom she faithfully served. "You need to understand something. The beguiling spirit we are dealing with is literally spellbinding and mesmerizing—a spirit so powerful that it has even deluded the one it so craftily uses."

"Rose?" Julie looked flabbergasted. "You mean the way she would look at me, drawing me into her world . . . you mean that was a *spirit*?"

Barbara nodded solemnly. Julie heard Jean suck in her breath. Barbara continued, "Christians certainly need to learn about the spiritual battle we are in. People are ignorant of Satan's devices." She sighed wearily, then added, "The beguiling spirit is one of the most powerful. It opens the door for other spirits to come in and oppress people. Usually, people end up with a soul tie, but they don't seem to be able to recognize it for what it is. But," she added triumphantly, "Praise be to God, He gives us overcoming power through the blood of Christ."

*There is so much to learn*, Julie thought. In fact, there was no end to learning. *Only God knows all, and we're certainly not God.* Julie stared at the tips of her white tennis shoes. "God dug out that soul tie, Barbara. Believe me, it was no fun. This whole experience was one expensive lesson! But," she said happily, "I've honestly forgiven her."

"I know it's hard," Barbara said with conviction, "But necessary. The Lord is gracious, and He is faithful to meet us where we're at." She set her empty pie plate on the coffee table in front of her. "Ummm, delicious. The best I've ever had!" She sipped her coffee and asked, "Where is Rose these days? Have you heard anything?"

Julie and Jean exchanged looks. "Well," Jean began, "She was in Arizona with her kids, but the last we heard, some woman who apparently has means from North Dakota bought her a new car and set her up in a small ministry up there."

"God help us," Barbara said softly. "I feel so sorry for those deluded people." She looked at Jean, then Julie. "Well, girls, it looks like you two have learned some valuable lessons which aren't taught in Bible school!" She chuckled briefly, then continued, "I've ministered in America and also Africa. I've been to Canada and to Mexico. But no matter where I've traveled, one truth remains—there is only one true Rose, and His name is Jesus."

A hallowed hush descended over the small gathering as each, with closed eyes, contemplated Barbara's final statement. *Is it just my imagination,* Julie wondered, *or did the others notice it too: the most heavenly perfume one could ever breathe. There's a sweet Presence here,* Julie thought, *Flooding the room with light and glory; flooding my heart and soul with waves of love, joy, and an ecstasy I've never experienced before.*

Then the aroma of frankincense and sweet spices came again, barely perceptible at first. It couldn't be an illusion this time; no, it was unmistakably noticeable. The aromatic, fragrant scent which has no equal in this material world lingered for long moments before gently withdrawing to be reunited with its invisible, yet Omnipresent Source—the Fairest One of all.

# EPILOGUE

God in His infinite wisdom had indeed put Julie and Jean together in a full-time ministry team that, in the ensuing years, carried out their commission of setting the captives free through teaching, preaching, counseling, and deliverance. A third Christian worker and gospel soloist was added to their team, forging a "three-fold cord that cannot be broken." In time, modern technology helped them to produce thousands of articles, Bible studies, and seventy books, including a discipleship course equal to four-years of Bible school that has been widely accepted in many third-world countries.

*"Faithful is he that calleth you,*
*who also will do it." – 1 Thessalonians 5:24*

# Books By Jeannette Haley

## Books co-authored with Rayola Kelley:
Hidden Manna (original)
The Many Faces of Christianity (Volume 6)
Post to Post 3: Meditations Along the Way
Post to Post 4: Inspirations Along the Way

## Other Books:
Angelus Assignments
(Interview in Hell & Interview on Earth)
The Pig and I
Reflections of Wonder (Devotional)

## Children's Books:
Little Stories for Little People
Traveler's Tales
The Adventures of Zack and Mira
The Adventures of Paul and Dana:
(A House on the Beach)
The Monster of Mystery Valley